THE DECEIVERS

ALFRED BESTER

A WALLABY BOOK
Published by Simon & Schuster
NEW YORK

THE DECEIVERS

All rights reserved
including the right of reproduction
in whole or in part in any form
Published by Wallaby Books
A Simon & Schuster Division of
Gulf & Western Corporation
Simon & Schuster Building
1230 Avenue of the Americas
New York, New York 10020

WALLABY and colophon are registered
trademarks of Simon & Schuster

First Wallaby Books Printing 1981
Published by arrangement with Tom Doherty Associates
10 9 8 7 6 5 4 3 2 1
Manufactured in the United States of America

Cover art by Michael Whelan
Interior illustrations by Rick DeMarco

ISBN 0-671-43432-2

TABLE OF CONTENTS

Chapter One

DISCOVERY

I do not know what I may appear to the world, but to myself I seem to have been only like a boy playing on the seashore and diverting myself in now and then finding a smoother pebble or a prettier shell than ordinary, whilst the great ocean of truth lay all undiscovered before me.

—Isaac Newton

He was wearing a jumpsuit of radiation armor, colored white, signifying executive level. He wore a white helmet with the visor down. He was armed, as all executives were in this quasi-military installation. He walked statelily across the floodlit concrete plain toward the giant hangar looming in the night. His control seemed to be massive.

At the towering hangar, shaped like a domed observatory, a squad of black-armored guards lay dozing before an entry hatch. The executive kicked the sergeant brutally but quite dispassionately. The squad leader exclaimed and scrambled to his feet, followed by the rest of his men. They opened the hatch for the man in white who stepped through into pitch black. Then, almost as an afterthought, he turned back into the light, contemplated the squad standing fearfully at attention and, quite dispassionately, shot their sergeant.

There was no light inside the hangar, only sound. The executive spoke quietly in the darkness.

"What is your name?"

The reply was a sequence of binary bits, treble blips and bass beeps. "--' ' '--' '---'--"

"Not in binary. Switch to phonetics. RW What is your name? RR answer."

The answer was as quiet as the question; but it was not a single voice, it was a chorus of voices speaking in unison. "Our name is R-OG-OR 1001."

"What is your mission, Rogor?"

"To obey."

"To obey what?"

"Our program."

"Have you been programmed?"

"Yes."

"What is your program?"

"Convey passengers and freight to OxCam University Dome on Mars."

"Will you receive commands?"

"Only from authorized control."

"Am I authorized?"

"Your voice print has been programmed into the command bank. Yes."

"I.D. me."

"We identify you as Executive Level One."

"My name?"

The reply was again a series of high-low bits.

"That is my statistical I.D. What is my social name?"

"It has not been entered."

"You will receive it now and link it to my voice print."

"Circuits open."

"I am Doctor Damon Krupp."

"Received. Entered. Linked."

"Are you programmed for inspection?"

"Yes, Doctor Krupp."

"Open for inspection."

The hangar dome slowly split into two hemispheres which slid down and admitted the soft light of the starry sky, revealing the two-man craft with which Krupp had been speaking. Standing tall over the deep ignition pit, it bore a startling resemblance to a giant antique Russian samovar; small crown head, wide cylindrical body with what might have been odd handles thrusting out, then tapering to a square base on four feet which actually were jet nozzles.

A hatch opened at the base, flooding the hangar with light from the craft's interior—the ship had no need for portholes—and Krupp stepped up two inset rungs and entered to inspect. R-OG-OR 1001 was surprisingly overheated. Krupp stripped off his clothes and crawled and clung his way up toward the control deck which was the samovar crown. (There would be no such climbing. constraint out in weightless space.) In the main belly cabin he discovered the reason for the tropical heat; a naked woman was sweating and swearing over the maintenance gear surrounding a transparent incubator. She was tinkering and crawling over and under the complications like an octopus.

It was his assistant, Dr. Cluny Decco, and Krupp had never seen her nude before, but his controlled voice did not betray his delighted amazement.

"Cluny?"

"Yeah, Damon. I heard you and the ship

exchanging compliments. Ouch! Goddamn!"

"Trouble?"

"This sonofabitch oxygen feed is temperamental. Now you see it, now you don't. It may kill the kid."

"We won't let it."

"We can't take any chances. After seven months of the care and feeding of our fetus, I'm not going to have a piece of machinery blow it for us."

"It's not the gear, Cluny, it's ambient pressure that's throwing off readings and choking the feed. The gear was designed for space, and space will make all the difference."

"And if it doesn't?"

"Then we crack the crib and give the boy mouth-to-mouth."

"Crack this thing? Christ, Damon, it'd take a sledge to split it open."

"Don't be so literal, Cluny. I meant crack it open procedurewise."

"Oh." She crawled out and stood up, steaming in skin and temper. Krupp had never seen her look so desirable. "Sorry. I never did have any sense, humorwise." She gave him a peculiar look. "Was the mouth-to-mouth a joke, too?"

"Not any more," Krupp said, seizing her. "I've been promising myself this as soon as our boy was decanted. He's born now, Cluny . . . "

And this is why R-OG-OR 1001 crashed on Ganymede.

The ship had been swung off-course by a lucky hit on the guidance system by a rare million Bev cosmic particle. This happens occasionally and is corrected manually, but Krupp and Decco had too much blind faith in computers and were too involved with their passion to check, so all three, the man, the woman, and the boy in the incubator, went down.

o   o   o

All this on Jekyll Island (no relation to Mr. Hyde) where the story began. I'm rather proud of this because it's unusual to discover the very first link in a chain of events. I'm not proud of the fact that I'm using 20-20 hindsight, since my business must be 20-20 foresight. You'll find out why later on in the chain.

I'm Odessa Partridge, and I was in a unique position to ferret out and sometimes reconstruct the events before and after the facts and put them in proper sequence in this telling. *Exempli gratia:* I began with the encounter in R-OG-OR 1001 which I didn't unearth until long afterward, mostly from the gossip still current at Cosmotron Gesellschaft. That answered a lot of questions much too late. Anyway, it was only a fringe benefit; I was after something else.

By the way, if I seem to be flip in my attitude, it's because my business can be so damned grueling that humor is the only sovereign remedy. God knows, the grim patterns generated on Jekyll Island which tortured the lives of the Synergist from Ganymede, the Sprite from Titania, and my own, needed all the humor I possessed.

Now let's have a look at the events surrounding

that first link in the chain.

When Cosmotron set up their Metastasis Energy Plant they threatened, blackmailed, bribed and finally were permitted to buy Jekyll Island on the Georgia coast. It took them a year to roust out and even kill off the squatters and dedicated ecologists entrenched in the Greenbelt preserve. It took them that same year to clean up the trash, garbage and corpses deposited by transients. Then they encircled Jekyll Island with 1,500 megavolts of electrified privacy and built their energy plant.

For the production they required apparatus long abandoned and forgotten. Another year was spent exploring and raiding museums for antique gear. Then they discovered that the brilliant young engineering Ph.Ds hadn't the foggiest notion of how to handle these antiquities. They hired a high-level personnel expert who heisted ancient professor-types out of retirement and put them under contract to operate the *apparat* which they alone could understand. The expert was elevated to supervisor status. He was Dr. Damon Krupp who had taken his degrees in Persona Analysis.

Krupp's doctoral dissertation had been on Huntington's chorea (Saint Vitus' Dance), a dazzling exploration of the concept that the disease magnified the intellectual and creative potential of the victim. It was so dramatic and caused such a stir that backbiters used to say, "Krupp has Huntington's chorea and Huntington has Krupp's."

He was still hipped on magnification of the intellect and the Cosmotron plant opened the door for a dangerous experiment. Cosmotron synthesized every element in the periodic table from atomic weights 1.008 (Hydrogen) to 259.59 (Asimovium) by a metastastic process which duplicated in miniature the solar thermonuclear caper. Radiation by-products were a constant problem, which is why the staff was required to wear armor at all times; but the radiation inspired Krupp's experiment, Maser Generated Fetal Amplification by Syndetic Emission of Radiation.

His assistant, Cluny Decco, was an M.D. and was delighted to participate, mostly because she was slavishly in love with Krupp, partly because she loved playing with machinery. Together they designed and set up the lab gear for what they called "The Magfaser Experiment," which, of course, was the acronym for Maser Generated Fetal, etc. Then came the problem of materiel. Here Cluny delivered.

She placed guarded advertisements in the Georgia media which, to the harassed alone, meant free abortions. Together, they examined all applicants, physically and psychologically, until the ideal one came along. She was a tall, dark, handsome mountain girl with a keen illiterate intelligence, the victim of a rural rape, two months pregnant. This time, Dr. Decco took extra pains to preserve the fetus intact in its sac which was placed in an amniotic fluid in a flask.

Cluny's microsurgery linking the umbilical cord to a balanced nutrient supply had been, by then, so explicitly researched that it was almost Standard Operational Procedure, but the tricky Maser amplification was the first ever. How it was done will never be known because only Krupp and Decco knew it and the secret died with them on Ganymede. However, Cluny had had a brief encounter with one of the Cosmotron executives, who must remain anonymous, and he reported this conversation from the bed.

"Listen, Cluny, you and Dr. Krupp have been overheard whispering about something you call 'Magfaser.' What is it?"

"An acronym."

"For what?"

"You've been very nice to me."

"Likewise, I'm sure."

"So can I put you on exec's honor?"

"I am already."

"No tell no one?"

"Not even President Gesellschaft himself."

"Maser generated fetal amplification by syndetic emission of radiation."

"What!"

"Yeah. We've been using some of our radiation by-products."

"To do what?"

"Amplify a fetus during gestation."

"A fetus! Inside you?"

"Hell no. It's a test-tube baby floating in a Maser womb. It's about nine months ready to decant now."

"Where'd you get it?"

"Even if I knew her name I wouldn't tell you."

"What are you amplifying it into?"

"That's the headache, we don't know. Damon

thought we were doing an overall amplification, sort of putting the kid through a magnifying glass . . . "

"Sizewise?"

"Brainwise, but we've been monitoring his dream patterns—you know that the fetus does dream, sucks its thumb and all that—and they're just average. Now we suspect that what we did was multiply a single aptitude by itself into a kind of quadratic X-square."

"Crazy!"

"So what's X, the unknown quantity, that's been multiplied by itself? Your guess is as good as mine."

"D'you think you'll find out?"

"Damon thinks we'd better get help. He's a brilliant guy, really the greatest, and what makes him great is his modesty. He's willing to admit when he's licked."

"Where will you find help?"

"We're taking a leave and jetting the kid to Mars, the OxCam University Dome. They're all spaced-out experts there and Damon has enough clout to get all the prognosis he needs."

"And all this for a test-tube experiment?"

"Man, this isn't just another experiment. This can't be just another test-tube baby, not after seven months of syndetic saturation. The kid must have some special quality, but what? Ah re-peats, suh. Yoah guess is as good as mine."

She never found out.

o   o   o

I saw a charming musical years ago in which the
compère (she was billed as "The Speakerine") not
only told the story and described the offstage
action, but also pitched in and played and sang a
dozen different roles. I feel very much like her
now because before I play Cupid in the romance of
the Sprite from Titania and the Synergist from
Ganymede, I've got to double as the Historian
(Historine?) of the whole solar picture.

Of course we've forgotten our history. That profound philosopher, Santayana (1863-1952) once
said, "Those who cannot remember the past are
condemned to repeat it." Surprise! Surprise!
We're repeating it with a stupidity that verges on a
death-wish. Let me recall the saga of our Solar,
just in case you cut that Monday lecture in
Cosmography or else dropped out entire because
you signed up for it by mistake, getting it confused
with Cosmetology 101—*The branch of philosophy
concerning itself with the general structure of
beautifying the complexion, skin, etc.* (2 credits)

It's the "New World" all over again. Just as the
English, Spanish, Portuguese, French and Dutch
had colonized the Americas and fought in the 17th
century, so the Terrans had colonized the Solar
and are now wrangling in the 27th century. A
thousand years don't change human nature much.
Nothing can. Consult your friendly neighborhood
anthropologist.

The Wops (to quote the Wasps) had a lock on
Venus. It was Italian and they insisted on calling it

"Venucci," in honor of Amerigo Vespucci, who had also given his name to some other place. Terra's moon, Luna, was quintessential California ("Like man, that sun! Gigsville like wow, hey!") and you would swear that any one of its demented Domes was Muscle Beach or Big Sur. Terra itself had been inherited by the old-fashioned Wasp Corridor after almost everybody else got the hell off.

The English found Mars closest to their native repellent climate, and the UK Domes were programmed for "Bright Periods," "Showers," and a Charles Dickens "White Christmas." One amusing aspect: The Martian "year" is nearly twice as long as the Terran year, which meant they had to go the twenty-four month route or opt for a sixty-day month. Nobody agreed, so there was hell to pay on Christmas, Easter, and Yom Kippur.

I'm simplifying, you understand. Actually, it's only the majority on Mars that's English. There are also the Welsh, Scots, Irish, Hindus, Nova Scotian, and even Appalachian mountaineers, descendants of the 17th-century English settlers in America. Some mingle with others; some prefer insularity.

Similarly, when I speak of Luna as "quintessential California," I'm really only describing the mad charm of that segment which has captivated all the Domes; Mexican, Japanese-American, Canadian, and even Vegas and Monte Carlo, the gaming centers. They've turned them on to bikinis, Lunar dune-buggies, holistic health, reflexology, and hot-tub babble about "human potential," "interface," and "what space you're into."

Keep that in mind while I describe the Solar. I'm merely highlighting the predominant in a galli-maufry.

Neptune's Triton, largest and remotest habitable satellite in the Solar, was Japanese-Chinese, contracted to "Jap-Chink" and "Jink," although there were other Asiatic races. They were as arrogant as ever, contemptuous of what they called "The Inner Barbarians," and now even more so since their discovery of "Meta" (short for metastasis) the amazing new energy generator which burst on the Solar like a thunderclap and ignited more conflicts than the entire history of gold.

We'd wasted our energy sources like drunken sailors for centuries and were down to an incredibly expensive scraping of the bottom of the barrel:

Quasi-fossil and semifossil fuels like peat and oil-bearing shales.

Sun, wind, and tide power. (Installations too complex and costly, except for the wealthy.)

Unburned carbons; soot, chimney sweepings, sulfur-bearing residues.

BTUs from machinery exhausts.

Friction heat from the rubber and plywood industries and plastics plants.

Fast-growing pulpwood forests; poplar, willow, and cottonwood. (But the population explosion had limited available acreage.)

Geothermal heat.

The Three Mile Island-type atomic-power generators were still being fought and blocked by half the population which would rather freeze than burn. Then along came Meta, the unexpected energy catalyst discovered on Triton, and it was almost as though Mother Nature had said, "If you've learned your lesson about waste, here's your salvation *if* you use it wisely."

Whether the Solar did remains to be seen.

Jupiter's Ganymede was strongly Afro, seasoned with Brown and mixed Mulatto. It had been taken over by the Blacks from France and her colonies who'd sickened of the hopeless war with the Honks and were now warring with themselves. (They're not primitive; just thorny.) Other Blacks and Browns were also lending a hand; Congo v. Tanzania, Maori v. Hawaii, Kenya v. Ethiopia, Alabama v. All-Africa, *und so weiter*. It was the despair of the **SAACP**, the Solar Association for the Advancement of the Colored People.

The Afro Domes are colorful and much visited by tourists. An attempt is made to replicate the tribal villages with palm-thatched huts (containing modern plumbing) and little yards with African animals for pets; nilgai, gnu, baby elephants and rhino, all sorts of exotic snakes, and even crocodiles (if you can afford a pond) which are a constant source of exasperation. Young crocs make gourmet eating for some, and the despicable crime of crocnapping has spread on

Ganymede.

The Dutch, plus others, were on Jupiter's
Callisto which, like Ganymede, is even bigger than
Mercury. Their Domes are reminiscent of
medieval Bruges, with cobbled streets and over-
hanging houses. (The Callisto Chamber of
Commerce won't like this, but the local whores,
like their predecessors in Amsterdam, still hang
small mirrors on either side of their windows for a
full view of the length of the street, and tap-tap-tap
the glass pane with a coin whenever a likely john
passes by.)

Callisto is heavy in the gold, silver, jewel and
gem-cutting business which has brought a large
Jewish population to the Domes. The Jews are
traditional experts with gems, and have always
been on traditionally friendly terms with the
Dutch. There are also the traditional artists'
colonies, and the rest of the Solar wonders how
painters with names like Rembrandt-29-van Rijn
or Jan-31-Vermeer dast demand and get so much
loot for *avant-garde* productions to which no
sensible person would give house-room.

Saturn's Titan (not to be confused with Uranus'
Titania, about which much more later) started like
England's old Australia. It was a dumping ground
for hopeless recidivists until the Solar decided
that it was cheaper to execute than transport, and
to hell with the do-gooders and bleeding hearts.
Titan descendants still speak an anachronistic,
incomprehensible convicts' jargon, is a lopsided
inferno of ancient hatreds against the Solar, and
plays no part in this faithful history except to

provide the classic line, "First prize, a day on Titan; second prize, a week on Titan."

Some of the small satellites like Phobos, Mimas, and Jupiter VI and VII have tiny freak colonies devoted to various religions, theater groups, diets, and sexual abstinences. With one lovely, extraordinary exception, no local inhabitants had ever been discovered on the solar planets and satellites, so the Dutch didn't have to buy Callisto for $24. No Indian wars against the English on Mars. Some clown calling himself "Star-born Jones" had started a cult for a thousand more who also believed that as infants they had been secretly kidnapped from Outer Space by the Solar. He established a JonesDome in the Caloris Basin on Mercury, which nobody wanted anyway.

A Mercurian "day" lasts 88 Terran days and the temperature soars high enough to melt lead. There was no need for the aliens snatched from the stars to commit suicide; the Dome insulation failed one day and they all roasted to death. The sort of sadists who relish the horrors of Grand Guignol theater often tour JonesDome to stare at the roasted, frozen mummies. One creep with a sick sense of humor stuck an apple in Star-born Jones' mouth. It's still there.

Ah, but that one extraordinary exception, Titania, the sprite of the unexpected, daughter of Uranus, mythic Ruler of the Heavens. Here were found local natives indeed! The great William Herschel, professional musician and amateur astronomer, sort of stumbled on Uranus with his homemade telescope back in 1781 and spotted the satellite Titania six years later. Are there any questions?

Q: Yes, we would like a description, please.

A: Well, Uranus is covered with very bright cloud bands of orange, red, and—

Q: Not Uranus, Titania.

A: Ah, yes, the magic moon. You know, the Cosmos must have a sense of humor. To almost every one of its systems or combinations a "Drop of Freak" is added to thumb its nose at order and harmony. It rather reminds one of Roger Bacon's famous line, "There is no excellent beauty that hath not some strangeness in the proportion."

Q: Francis.

A: What?

Q: Not Roger, Francis Bacon.

A: Francis, of course. Thank you. In the Solar assemblage, Titania is that strangeness, to the wonderment and exasperation of all the rest; wonderment because the few clues and hints we have are a fascinating exasperation because we can't understand them.

Q: What are they?

A: If you're acquainted with gems and crystals, you know that just about any crystal may have fluid inclusions. In size, inclusions range from a diameter of less than one micron to a few centimeters. Inclusions bigger than a millimeter in diameter are rather rare; those in the centimeter range are museum pieces.

Q: But don't they destroy the value of gems?

A: True. True, but we're exploring the geology of crystals. Most of their inclusions contain a solution of various salts in various concentrations from nearly pure water to concentrated brine. Most also enclose a bubble of gas. When the bubble is small enough to respond to irregularities in the number of molecules striking it, it can be seen to wander continuously in a jerky Brownian movement:

$$\frac{n^1}{n^2} = \exp\left[\frac{mg\,(p\text{-}p')\,No\,(h_1\text{-}h_2)}{pRT}\right]$$

Q: You lost us. Did you know?

A: Sorry. I just threw in a little classy Einstein, but, you know, it's fascinating to watch such a bubble under the microscope and to think that it's been nervously pacing its cell for a billion years.

Q: When are you getting to Titania, the magic moon?

A: Wait for it. Wait for it. Some inclusions have one or more crystals in their liquid; some are composed of several immiscible liquids; a few contain gas alone. Sometimes the crystals within the inclusion have their own fluid inclusions with bubbles in them, and so *ad infinitum*. Now, multiply this by a thousand miles, her diameter, and you have Titania, the freak of the Solar.

Q: What!

A: Indeed yes. Under the crust of meteoric trash and rubble accumulated through the eons, the satellite contains a conglomerate of giant crystals ranging from a foot to a mile in diameter.

Q: You ask us to believe that?

A: Why not? The traditional models of planets and satellites are being revised. It's speculated that Terra may actually be a living organism; we just can't go deep enough to find out. We do know that a hell of a lot more went into the formation of the Solar than gases condensing into mere solids.

Q: And what about Titania's crystals?

A: They have a multitude of inclusions and inclusions within inclusions, *ad infinitum.*

Q: And are they supposed to be alive, too?

A: We don't know, but we do know that they contain a fascinating life-form that has evolved, displaying its own Brownian movement. They're wonderful and perplexing and exasperating because they won't let the Solar visit and explore. "Titania for the Titanians," is their slogan.

Q: What do they look like?

A: The inclusions? A sort of proto-universe. They're self-illuminating and sometimes syncopate or synchronize when you jet close enough to make them out through the crust. There seems to be some sort of molecular or osmotic linkage between them which—

Q: No, no. The locals. The natives of Titania. What do you look like?

A: Oh, the Titanians. What do they look like? Italian, English, French, Chinese, Black, Brown, your wife, your husband, three lovers, two dentists, and a partridge in a pear tree.

Q: Don't joke. What do they look like?

A: Who's joking? They look like any living

thing. The Titanians are polymorphs, which means they can take any damn shape they please.

Q: And any sex?

A: No. Boys are boys and girls are girls, and they don't reproduce by budding.

Q: Is it an alien culture?

A: It's alien but not from a distant star. It's strictly a home-grown Solar product, but man like it's a race apart.

Q: Is it an ancient culture?

A: Dating back to the Terran Tertiary at least; around fifty million years.

Q: Is it a primitive culture?

A: No. It's advanced out of sight.

Q: Then why haven't the Titanians visited our earth in the past?

A: And what makes you think they haven't? King Tutankhamen could have been a Titanian. Or Pocahontas. Or Einstein. Or Rin-tin-tin. Or the mad scientist's Giant Clam That Clobbered Cuba. Or do I mean the giant scientist's Mad Clam?

Q: What! Are they dangerous?

A: No, they're full of fun and games. You never know what they're up to next. They're sprites of the unexpected.

And one of them fell in love with the Synergist.

o   o   o

We'd been tailing and using the Synergist, without his knowledge, for several years as a kind of hunting dog; in fact, our code name for him was "Pointer." You'll want to know how we used him.

Here's an example.

The Solar was being flooded with counterfeit coins and tokens, beautiful jobs minted from Britannia metal. We perted the operation—Pert is the acronym for Program Evaluation and Review Technique—put together a flow chart of the progress of the fakes from Mars out into the Solar, but we couldn't locate the Critical Path to attack. In other words, we had to find *the* one line in the network through which alone we could stop everything.

Well, "Pointer" was in the London Dome doing a Cockney color feature for *Solar Media*. He explored all the patterns, including the traditional Cockney Rhyming Slang; "plates" for "feet"— plates of meat, feet; "frog" for "road"—frog and toad, road; "titfer" for "hat"—tit for tat, hat; "dot" for "flash" (flash is counterfeit money)— dot and dash, flash. And *that* was our Critical Path.

Because there was an antique shop in New Strand called "Dot and Dash" which specialized in old medals, old silver loving cups, ornamental presentation swords, fancy gavels and maces . . . that sort of thing. Very chic. Very expensive. We'd been combing the metal foundries for the source of the coins without success; and here it was, right under our nose, unconsciously pointed out for us. Old loving cups aren't silver; they're Britannia metal.

We knew a lot about "Pointer," we had to, but we didn't know what breed he really was—he didn't know himself—and I'd best explain the enigma by describing my first meeting with him some time after we'd discovered that we could use his unique qualities.

It was at one of Jay Yael's delightful talk-ins. Jay is a professional art mavin and he collects people the same way he collects pictures. There were a dozen guests, including Yael's prized protégé, the Synergist. He was a tallish, angular, formerly-young man who somehow gave the impression that he would have been more comfortable without clothes.

He behaved like the rare, better sort of celebrity, and he *was* somewhat celebrated; balanced, amused, never taking himself seriously, clearly showing his feeling that fame is only part earned and mostly luck. And he had an extravagant sense of humor.

He displayed an absorbed interest in everybody and everything, listening intently and timing his responses to encourage speakers and draw them out. The timing was his synergic genius, but he had another remarkable quality; the ability to convince each separate member of a group that his absorbed interest was devoted solely to him- or herself. He made eye-contact and his glances said that you were the only one who really counted.

When people are poised and successful there's always the danger of inspiring hostility unless it can be seen that they're not altogether perfect. The Synergist had private flaws, to be sure, but also a public one which was curious and arresting. He wore enormous black-rimmed spectacles in an attempt to conceal the astonishing sunbursts scarred on his cheeks. He had a habit of pulling the spectacles down to mask the scars, so automatic that it was almost a tic.

He was Rogue Winter, of course, and during a lull in the conversation-pit I asked him whether his first name was a nickname. This merely to pique him into talking, you understand. I knew all about him because that was part of my job.

"No," he said solemnly. "It's short for Rogue Elephant. Dr. Yael discovered me in Africa, where he shot my mother. She'd been crossed with a gorilla by an alien breeder from Boötes alpha." He pulled the spectacles down. "No, I'm a liar. It's really short for Rogue Male. Dr. Yael discovered me in a whorehouse where he shot the madam. Dear Madam Bruce," he added wistfully. "He was like a mother to me." Spectacles. "But if you must have the *vero* truth," he said in deadly earnest, "my full name is Rogue's Gallery Winter. After Dr. Yael shot the Chief Inspector at Scotland Yard, he—"

"Oh stop it, son," Yael laughed. We were all laughing. "Tell the nice lady how I made my greatest discovery."

"I don't know about the great-bit, sir, but it was your discovery and it's your story. Damned if I'm going to *goniff* into your act."

"Yes, I raised you genteel-like," Yael smiled. "Well, briefly, Rogue'd been found in the wreckage of a craft by scouts from the Maori Dome on Ganymede. He was an infant, the only survivor, and they brought him back to the Dome, where the King or Chief, Te Uinta, formally adopted him."

"He had no sons," Winter explained, "only daughters. When Uinta dies, I get to be king banana."

"Hence the blazon of royalty on Rogue's cheeks, of which he's so absurdly ashamed."

"They kind of zig girls off into a zag," Winter said. Spectacles again.

Knowing his track record with women, I had to stifle a laugh, and I'm almost certain that his quick eye caught it.

"The Maori named him Rog," Yael continued, "because those were the only I.D. letters that could be made out on the wreck. R-dash-oh-gee. R-OG Uinta, pronounced with a long 'O' as in Rogue. Right, son?"

"Sounded more like R-grunt-O, sir," Winter said and pronounced his name Maori-style. "Makes people want to say, 'Gesundheit.'"

"End of part one," Yael went on. "Part two. I was visiting the Maori Dome to have a look at their wonderful woodcarving and came across this ten-year-old kid with his sister. She was wearing a beaded tunic and he was pointing to the beads and trying to explain a pattern he saw in them."

"Which was?" I asked.

"Tell the nice lady, R-grunt-G."

"It seemed so obvious." Winter pulled the specs down. "The pattern was beads and stitches in a triangle:

Red-Red-Red-Red-Red-Red-Red-Red
Stitch-Stitch-Stitch-Stitch
Black-Black
Stitch."

Yael rolled his eyes to heaven. "God deliver

mere mortals from a genius!" he laughed. "Did
you hear him speaking triangle? He will do that;
he thinks and lives patterns. I'll have to translate.
The king's child was pointing to a group of eight
red beads and holding up one finger. Then he
pointed to four empty stitches and made Maori
sign for zero. One finger up for two black beads.
Zero sign for the single empty stitch. Then he
swept his palm across the triangle and held up ten
fingers. His sister giggled because she was
ticklish, and that was my discovery."

"What?" I asked. "That girls are ticklish?"

"Of course not. That her brother was a genius."

"At beadwork design?"

"Sharpen a wit, madame. One group of eight. No
four. One two. No units. The king's child was
counting in binary. One-oh-one-oh equals ten."

"It seemed so obvious," Winter repeated.

"What? Obvious?" Yael snorted. "A naked,
illiterate Maori kid discovering binary on his
own? Well, naturally I made a deal with King Te
Uinta, brought R-grunt-G back to Terra, Englished
his name to Rogue Winter, began his education,
and then had a problem. Where the devil do you
aim a child with a genius for patterns?"

"Math?" I suggested.

"That came second. With my bias, art came
first, but after a brilliant start in Paris the boy lost
interest and damped off. Then math at M.I.T. and
the same thing. Architecture at Princeton, business at Harvard, Juilliard for music, Cornell Med,
Taliesin for Dome design, astrophysics at
Palomar—all the same story; brilliant start and

then a damping off of dedication."

"They all seemed compartmentalized," Winter said. "Parts of a whole without any connection. I was looking for the whole ball of wax."

"He was of age by now, so I drove him out—"

"With whips," Winter cringed.

"With a thousand in his pocket for a *Wanderjahr,* and stern orders not to return until he'd discovered what he wanted to do with himself. Frankly, I expected him to come crawling back, dead broke and obedient . . . "

"Like a rogue and peasant slave."

"What's that cribbed from?" I asked Winter.

"*Hamlet,* Act 2, Scene 2," he whispered. "Don't tell anyone, but I studied English Lit. behind Yael's back. You know, *Major British Writers I & II.* Busted that too," he added, "owing to a surfeit of lampreys."

"Instead, the young man swaggered in, if you please, with cash bursting out of his jumpsuit and the tape of the damnedest integration the Solar has ever seen. You all must recall 'Lockstep,' a best-seller. Rogue wove gambling on Luna with—"

"I ran the doctor's gift up to a hundred thousand before word got around and they barred me from the casino tables," Winter laughed. "Rogue the Greek, they called me."

"—with corn crops in Kansas, Meta on Triton, high fashion on Ganymede, the Women's Movement on Venucci, art auctions on Callisto— all into a Solar pattern which he made so obvious but which had never been noticed before. He'd found himself, by God! He was a Synergist."

Chapter Two

THE SPRITE AND THE SYNERGIST

synergy (*sin er·ji*), *n.* Combined action or operation. Cooperative action of discrete agencies such that the total effect is greater than the sum of the effects taken independently.
> —Noah Webster, 1758-1843

The synergic sense in Rogue Winter was not an overall resonance to every pattern and construct; he had odd deaf/blind spots, many trivial, a few serious. Most serious was the fact that he responded to the patterns of three languages but was only conscious of relating to two. This is what plunged him into disaster.

Winter spoke Solar-Verbal because he was an Inquisitor (back in the twentieth century they called it an "Investigative Reporter") and the words of the worlds were the tools of his trade. He knew he understood Soma-Gestalt (back in the twentieth century they called it "body English") because he'd had much investigating experience communicating with strangers on many levels, and it was his business to discover what realities lay hidden behind the concealment of words.

All this he knew, but what he didn't know was that he resonated to the Anima Mundi which produced his extraordinary synergic pattern sense. I used to think that the frightful shock to the infant of the crash of the R-OG craft was the cause of his hypersynsitivity. Now I know that it was the

Krupp-Decco matter experiment, and the X-quantity which was multiplied by itself in Rogue was what I call a "Phane Sense," from the Greek, *phainein*, meaning to show. It was this phane sense that enabled him to be shown things from apparently unrelated facts and events and synergize them into a whole.

Anima Mundi is the fundamental "Soul of the World." Latinwise, *Anima* = soul life. *Mundi* = the world. Anima Mundi is the cosmic spirit pervading all living things and, it is argued, even all inanimate things as well. I believe that myself. An old house has a spirit and character of its own. How often have you seen a picture which doesn't like its place in the decor and rebels by refusing to hang straight? Don't chairs poke us for attention as we pass, and sulky stair treads trip us up?

So many of us resonate to Anima and are powerfully influenced by it. We can recognize some obvious aspects; "soul," "vibes," "Psi," weather and night-and-day affects; but we don't realize that these are merely facets of the deep, underlying Anima Mundi which is the bedrock, so to speak, the bottom line of all existence. Rogue Winter understood this least of all while he was being affected most of all. Here's an instance of his unconscious response to the bedrock patterns, which we got from the Flemish girl.

He was on assignment on Mars and taking an afternoon off fishing a salt lake in the Welsh Dome. They'd stocked it with Coelacanths, "Old Four-Legs," a legacy from the Cretaceous. Winter was casting and retrieving his lure, fishing east to meet the schools of Four-Legs feeding from east to west. Suddenly—he thought it was a hunch, he thought he was outsmarting the fish, but it was really his unconscious seventh sense forcing him to answer an Anima command—suddenly he reversed himself and began fishing west.

After he'd been casting without success for a few minutes, a girl appeared on the lonely lakeshore. She was wearing chopped jeans, no top, had swept bronze hair, and was carrying two heavy shopping totes without benefit of null-G. She put them down, rubbed her arms, smiled and said, "Allo."

He was instantly enchanted by her French accent and grateful that she didn't stare at the sunbursts blazoned on his cheeks. "Good evening. Where are you going?"

"I am guest at 'ouse in next village. I 'ave been buying *dineur*."

"Where are you visiting from?"

"Callisto."

"But I thought Callisto was Dutch."

"You 'ave never *visite?*"

"Not yet."

"Is not all *Hollandais*. Is Benelux, *comprenez?* Is also Flanders, Belgium, Luxembourg. I am from Flemish Dome. You are feeshing?"

"As you see. Would you like a fish for *dineur?*" He reeled in and held the lure up to her. "Spit on it and that will bring us luck." That was a lie, of course, but she was very pretty and had a delicious bosom.

She gave him a perplexed look, was reassured by his gallant glance, and spat delicately on the lure. Winter cast out into the deeper waters, started his jig-jag retrieve, and had a tremendous strike. He couldn't believe his luck. He shouted with laughter and began fighting to bring the fish in while the girl danced excitedly alongside him. He kept a tight line on the Four-Legs but when at last he brought it to shore it was the body of a child.

The Flemish girl moaned, "*Dieu!* Is the Megan *fille.* She drown this afternoon. They 'ave look for 'er bodee ever since."

"Jesus Jig God," Winter muttered. He detached the lure from the tiny bathing suit and picked up the body. "Show me where to take her."

He hadn't the faintest inkling that it was a subliminal summons by the Anima to which his synsitivity had responded. There was an unbalanced death that had to be fitted into the Anima pattern, and it called him west. It might have been resolved eventually by other natural responses, but Rogue Winter's seventh sense, his resonance to the bottom line, had drawn him there first.

And he hadn't the faintest inkling that it was this same Anima resonance which produced the serendipity which always amazed and amused him. Serendipity is the faculty of making unexpected and unsought discoveries by accident. You're on your way from A to B, minding your own business, and you stub your toe on X, much like Herschel stumbling on Uranus. This was the quality that made Rogue Winter our "Pointer."

What else on him from our Meta file (MAX SECRET. ALEPH AGENTS ONLY) *Operation Pointer:*

He had curious recall. He remembered shapes to the milli, but not colors. He could remember the argument and action of everything he had read or seen, but not addresses or phone numbers. He remembered the personality of everyone he had met, but not their names. He recalled his love affairs in patterns which the ladies would not appreciate.

He had undergone risky cerebral surgery to install prosthetic synapses which gave him a brain-wave interface with his studio computer. Winter could think to his workshop computer which would print, tape, and/or graphically illustrate his concepts. Not many can use this advanced technique. It demands an unswerving concentration which cannot be deflected by stray associations.

He would do anything to puzzle out the warp and woof of a pattern; lie, cheat, charm, steal, bully, humble himself, break any one of the Ten Commandments plus the Eleventh (Thou Shalt Not Get Caught) and he had broken most of them in the line of duty.

He was thirty-three years old, 6-1½, 187 lbs., in fair condition. Once upon a time he'd been married to a darling girl from the Frisco Dome on Luna. She wore her fair hair in a casque, had slitty dark eyes, a supple swimmer's body, and a big front, a type to which Winter was always attracted. She spiced every sentence with the ig-words that were the current cant of the Lunar Domes and are spreading: "Zig, man, I love you, gig? but I'm jig sleepy is all, gone to bed, mig."

Charming, flaky, entertaining, but, alas, merely with it in the I.Q. department, so the marriage broke up. Winter loved ladies, but only as equals. One of his ladies, also a slender-big-front-number, remarked bitterly that even he couldn't live up to his idea of equality. The Titanian sprite took care of that.

o   o   o

A change of life in a day of synergy.

Winter had returned from an assignment inquis-iting the Women's Movement on Venucci and he was still in shock from a violent event in the Bologna Dome; the more so because he couldn't understand it. This was the night before the day that changed his life.

He had a floor-through apartment in the *Beaux Arts* rotunda, a complex built in the old Edwardian style with bay windows, fireplaces, and thick walls for the protection of creative artists from each other. The insulation muffled the cries of sopranos coping with coloratura, the electronic thunder of "Galactic Gavotte in G-minor," the dictation of the Oxford English Dictionary being translated into Nü-Spēk.

His pad was old-fashioned and exactly suited to his taste: Large living room with Georgian furnish-ings, utility kitchen, bath with a monster six-foot tub, two bedrooms in the rear, one large, one small. The small resembled a monk's cell in its simplicity. The large was his workshop and a mess; walls lined with books, tapes, films, software; a conference table for a desk; the studio computer to which he was neurally linked—he had to make sure the read-in was switched off when not in use, otherwise it would record everything he was thinking in the apartment—stacks of stationery, virgin film and tape, shambles of old stories cluttering the floor, some spewing off their spools looking like a clutch of serpents in search of Laocoön and his two sons.

He was so upset that he didn't bother to unpack his travel tote or even change, and the Alitalia jets are not famed for cleanliness. Instead he got a whiskey bottle, sat down on the living-room couch with his feet up on the coffee table and tried to drink himself numb. He was trying to recover from his first killing, which had taken place his last night on Venucci.

Turning points occur in moments. This was a three-second affray in the dim Central Gardens of the Bologna Dome that changed Winter's life. He was waiting for a girl to keep her date with him when a gorill armed with a deadly knife came at him out of the dark bushes. Years of childhood drilling had trained Winter's reflexes. He did not meet force with force as was natural and expected; instead he went limp, fell supine, did a double-roll as the assailant floundered over him, and was on the killer's back. Two smashes with a knee into the testicles, knife-wrist twisted back and snapped with both hands, knife seized and right carotid slashed. All this in three seconds of hissing silence. It took the killer much longer to die. Winter didn't like to think of that.

"But why, baby? Why?" he kept asking.

Three drinks later he was suddenly inspired. "What I need right now is a girl to lose myself in. That's the only way to wait for a pattern to show."

One of his reciprocal Rogues (he had a dozen alternate selves) answered, "Feel free, but you left your big red book in the workshop."

"Why, for jigjeeze sake, can't I have the little black book, famed in song and story?"

"Why can't you remember a phone number? Never mind. Shall we join the ladies?"

He made three calls, all negative. He had three more drinks, all positive. He stripped, went to his Japanese bed in the monk's cell, thrashed, swore, and slept at last, dreaming crazed p a t t e r n s
                    a t t e r n s
                    t t e r n s
                    t e r n s
                    e r n s
                    r n s
                    n s
                    s

Next morning Winter was up fairly early and out. First to the network for a script conference with his producer. Next to his publisher for a battle over graphics. Last to *Solar Media* where he entered the editorial corridors and began his customary circus parade, kissing and pinching the staff without bias and finishing in Augustus

(Ching) Sterne's corner office. Ching was editor-in-chief.

"Have you got the story, Rogella?"

"Got it."

"Deadline in three weeks."

"I'll make it. Have you got an empty office I can use for an hour or so? I have to make some calls and production gave me my galleys to check. They want them back today."

"Which story is that?"

"Space And Mongolian Idiocy: Arrested Development in $E = Mc^2$."

"Crikey! That should have gone to the lab yesterday. Use the conference room, Rogella. Nobody's brainstorming in there today."

Winter settled down in the conference room, made his calls, rang the copy department to come pick up his Venucci reference material for their files, finger-read his author's galley tapes—electrotaxis was another facet of his synergic skills—flew into a rage, rang Ching Sterne and began to ream him out.

A girl poked her head into the conference room. It was a streaky blonde head with hair like a helmet and slitty dark eyes; Demi Jeroux from the copy department. Winter motioned her to enter, blew her a kiss and continued to swear venomously on the intercom. "I've been checking the galleys on the idiot piece and some sonofabitch has been rewriting my copy. How many times do I have to tell you? Nobody fucks around with my copy! You want changes, ask me and I'll make them. I won't let a shit-ass second-guesser climb onto my by-line."

Winter banged the intercom down, turned and beamed at the girl who looked frightened. "Demi, love, what a dear sight you are for a drinking man. Come on, give Daddy a big hug." He opened his arms and she trembled against him. "My peerless copy-checker, I've got all the Venucci background material for you."

"I'm not a copy-checker anymore," Demi said in a soft Virginia voice.

"Don't tell me they've fired my Gem of the Ocean."

"I was promoted. I'm a junior editor."

"Congratulations! And about time. They've been wasting a bright girl from— What was that cockagiggy college you took from?"

"Marymount."

"Did they give you a raise?"

"Alas."

"Shits! Never mind, we'll celebrate anyway. Come on out and I'll get you stoned."

"You won't want to, Rogue."

"Why not?"

"Well . . . my first assignment was— It was your Mongolian piece."

"You mean *you're* the sonofabitch who—? And you heard me hollering down the pipe?" Winter burst out laughing and kissed the girl, who blushed vividly. "You've had your first lesson in handling me. Will you be editing my Women's Lib inquisition?"

She nodded shyly. "I've been assigned to you. Mr. Sterne says it'll be educational."

"Now I wonder what he could possibly mean by

that? Well, well! Look at Demi Jeroux, the Dixie-
land Demon, now my editor."

The girl took a deep, shaky breath and sat down
on one of the conference chairs with a fetching
mixture of determination and terror. "I want to be
something else," she said in her soft voice.

"Oh?"

"Remember that story you told me about the
Irish houseparty?"

"No, dear."

"That time you took me to lunch at the Kosher
Space-Ahoy Seafood Grotto?"

"I remember the lunch but not the story."

"There . . . There was an infant crawling around
under everybody's feet and you got mad and
kicked him."

"Oh God! Gig!" Winter laughed. "It was in the
Dublin Dome. I'll never forget the shock of horror
that ran through the assembled. It was a rotten
thing to do, but it was such a damned dull party."

"And the infant looked at you with love."

"He did. He did. Liam must be eight years old by
now and he still loves me. He writes to me, in
Gaelic. It's almost as though he was born with a
mad passion to be kicked."

"Rogue," Demi said, "you've kicked me, too."

"I—? Kicked—?"

An amazed thrill prickled his skin. He'd been
propositioned before, but never quite like this.

Have I asked for it?

Did I invite it?

Is she aware of a two-way attraction that I never
sensed?

Am I lying?

Did I want this all along?

So his reciprocals quaeried while he got up,
closed the door of the conference room, came back
to the girl, pulled a chair around so that he could
face her knees to knees, and took her hands.

"What is it, Demi?" he asked gently. "Rotten old
love?"

She nodded and began to cry. He pulled out a
kerchief and put it in her hand.

"What a brave thing to say, darling. How long
has this been going on?"

"I don't know. It just . . . happened."

"Just now?"

"No, it— It just sort of happened."

"How old are you, love?"

"Twenty-three."

"Been in love before?"

"Never with anyone like you."

Winter looked at this weeping slender little
thing with a big front and sighed. "Listen to me,"
he said carefully. "In the first place, I'm grateful.
When someone offers love it's like the end of the
rainbow, and not many of us find that treasure. In
the second place, I could love you right back, but
you have to understand why, Demi. When love is
given, the response is love; it's a kind of beautiful
blackmail. I'm just distracting you with the
obvious so you won't get my kerchief too wet . . ."

"I know," she whispered. "You're always
honest."

"So I can be had. I'm queer for women—it's my
one vice—and now of all times I need a girl badly,
but—now you must look at me, Demi—but you'll

only have half a man . . . less, maybe. Most of me belongs to my work."

"That's why you're a genius," she said.

"Stop adoring me!" He stood up abruptly and crossed to a giant map of the Solar which he examined without interest. "My God! You're determined to harpoon me, aren't you."

"Yes, Rogue. I don't like it but . . . yes."

"Is there no mercy? The late, great Rogue Winter landed by a Marymount *nebbish*, proving yet again that I'm a clown who can say no to anybody except a girl."

"Are you afraid?"

"Damn right I am, but I'm helpless. All right, come on." He opened his arms to her and she fled into them. They kissed; merely a firm contact of lips from him.

"I love your hard mouth," she murmured. "And your hands are hard, too. Oh, Rogue . . . Rogue . . ."

"That's because I'm a Maori savage."

"Not you. There's no one like you, Rogue."

"Will you zig off the worship. I'm vain enough as it is."

"Golly! I never thought I'd get you."

"Yeah? Like hell!" Winter appealed to the ceiling. "Please, holy ancestors of the royal Uinta line, noble kings who have ruled the Maori for fifteen generations and whose souls now reside in Te Uinta's left eye . . . Please don't let me be gaffed by this black widow spider!"

Demi giggled and let out a Ssss! of delight.

"What can a noble savage do when a girl sets her

sights on him? He's surrounded, doomed, losted."

"Left eye?" Demi asked.

"Uh-huh. We believe that's where the souls dwell." He closed his right eye and the left returned her look of delight and anticipation. "Gigsville, Demi. Leave us go out and celebrate, only now it's me that's going to get smashed . . . to numb the pain."

"Ssss!"

o   o   o

Had we but world enough, and time, this coyness, lady, were no crime.
First she had to tour the apartment, inspecting and sometimes admiring every piece of furniture, every picture, every book and tape, the knickknacks and souvenirs of his assignments through the Solar. She raised an eyebrow in old-fashioned surprise at the six-foot tub (formerly illegal because such luxuries devoured too much energy before the Age of Meta), cocked an eye at the Japanesey bed, merely a thick white mattress on a giant slab of ebony, and let out a little moan at the mess in the workshop.
We would sit down, and think which way to walk, and pass our long love's day. Thou by the Indian Ganges side should'st rubies find; I by the tide of Humber would complain.

"What did you like about me?"

"When?"

"When I first came to work for *Solar*."

"What makes you think I liked you?"

"You took me to lunch."

"It was your dedication."

"To what, in particular?"

"To granting Vulcan its rightful place in the family of planets."

"There isn't any Vulcan."

"That's what I liked about you."

"What's this in the souvenir box, please?"

"It's a porcelain doll's face. I found it in a trash barrel in the Anglia Dome on Mars and fell madly in love with her."

"And this?"

"Oh come now, Demi. You don't really want to explore my entire past, do you?"

"No, but tell me, please. It's so odd."

"It's a teardrop from the Gem Tower in the Burma Dome on Ganymede."

"Gem Tower?"

"They pour synthetic jewels the same way they used to drop pellets in a shot tower centuries ago. They were pouring red ruby flux and this one didn't drop spherical, so they gave it to me."

"It's so strange. It looks like there's a flower inside it."

"Yes, that's a flaw. Would you like it?"

"No, thanks. I want more than flawed rubies from you."

"She's turning aggressive," Winter told the living room. "Now that she's nailed me, she's showing her true colors."

I would love you ten years before the Flood, and you should, if you please, refuse till the conversion of the Jews.

"And what did you like about *me* when you first met me at *Solar?*" he asked.

"Your beat."

"My exhaustion?"

"Gracious no! Your rhythm."

"That's because I'm really a Black. We all got rhythm."

"No you're not. You're not even a real Maori." She touched his cheek with tender fingertips. "I know how you got these scars."

He pulled his spectacle down.

"You do everything with some sort of beat," she went on. "Like a rhythm section in a combo. When you walk, talk, joke . . . "

"What are you, some kind of music freak?"

"So I wanted to get into your tempo."

As she replaced the ruby teardrop in the souvenir box, Winter stared. The evening light had caught her at an odd angle and suddenly she bore a flashing resemblance to the redheaded Rachel Straus of *Solar Media* with whom he'd once had a perplexing relationship.

My vegetable love should grow vaster than empires, and more slow.

He was beginning to feel uncomfortable with her; a new sensation for him. "This is a damned lymphatic start for anything," he complained.

"Why? Isn't it full of fun and games?"

"Who's having fun?"

"Me."

"Who's playing games?"

"Me."

"So where do I come in?"

"Just play it by ear."

"The left or the right?"

"The middle. That's where your soul dwells."

"You're the damnedest girl I've ever met."

"I've been berated by better men than you, sir."

"Like who?"

"Like the ones I refused."

"You leave me in doubt."

"Yes, that's the only way to handle you."

"Damn it, I'm outclassed," he muttered.

An hundred years should go to praise thine eyes, and on thy forehead gaze: two hundred to adore each breast: but thirty thousand to the rest; an age at least to every part, and the last age should show your heart.

"This is the last thing I expected from you," she smiled.

"What last thing?"

"Your being shy."

"Me? Shy!" He was indignant.

"Yes, and I like it. Your eyes are taking inventory, but the rest of you hasn't made a move."

"I deny that."

"Tell me what you see."

"A crazy kaleidoscope."

"Maybe you'd better explain."

"I—" He hesitated. "I can't. I— You always look different."

"How?"

"Well ... Your hair. Sometimes it looks straight, sometimes wavy, sometimes fair, other times dark ..."

"Oh, that's a new dye called 'Prisma.' It responds to wavelengths. You ought to see what an A.P.B. broadcast does . . . turns me into the Northern Lights."

"And your eyes. Sometimes they look dark and slitty, like my ex-wife's; other times they open up into huge opals . . . like a girl from the Flemish Dome I once knew."

"That's just a trick," she laughed. "All girls practice it. It's supposed to stagger men like a bolt of lightning." She pulled his spectacles off and put them on. "There. Feel safer now?"

"And— And the boozalum." He was close to stammering. "When you first came to work for us I thought they were . . . they were cute little points. Now they're—they're—Have you been growing up while I was out on assignments?"

"Let's see," she said, and started to remove her blouse.

But at my back I always hear time's winged chariot hurrying near: and yonder all before us lie deserts of vast eternity. Thy beauty shall no more be found; nor in thy marble vault, shall sound my echoing song: then worms shall try that long-preserved virginity, and your quaint honor turn to dust, and into ashes all my lust.

"Don't," he said. "Please don't."

"Why not? Still shy?"

"No, I—it's not what I expected."

"Of course not. The macho Maori. But *I'm* making the pass." The blouse came off. "How long d'you expect a girl to wait? Until she's in the grave?"

"Jigjeeze!" he exclaimed. "You look like a figurehead on the prow of a ship."

"Yes. They call me the China Clipper."

"What are you, some kind of Virgins' Lib militant?"

"Now why don't we find out?" she laughed. "Come on, Rogue . . ."

She hauled him off the couch and pulled him toward the bedroom with one hand while with the other she tore open his clothes.

Let us roll all our strength and all our sweetness up into one ball, and tear our pleasures with rough strife through the iron gates of life. Thus, though we cannot make our Sun stand still, yet we will make him run.

And yet she did make the sun stand still in a timeless lovers' limbo. In the darkness she seemed to be a hundred women with hundreds of hands, mouths, and loins. She was a Black with thick lips that engulfed him, and hard, high buttocks that clutched him. She was a Wasp virgin, supine, helpless, yet trembling with joy.

She was a succulent, crooning in his ear while her mouths drank arpeggios from his skin. She was an outworld animal emitting guttural grunts as he bestialized her. She became an inflated synthetic mannequin, squeaking and buzzing the sounds of a pinball machine. She was tough, tender, demanding, yielding, always unexpected.

And she inspired lurid fantasies in him. He was being whipped, crucified, drawn and quartered, branded with glowing irons. He thought he could see them together in impossible tangles reflected

in magnifying mirrors. He panicked as he heard
the front door being hammered while muffled
voices shouted threats. His loins seemed to mount
into a volcano of endless eruptions. Yet through
all this he imagined he was carrying on a sparkling
conversation with her over champagne and caviar
as an erotic prelude to lounging before the fire to
share love for the first time.

Chapter Three

ENERGIES

I am more and more convinced that man is a dangerous creature; and that power, whether vested in many or few, is ever grasping.

—Abigail Adams

Winter eased out of the Japanese bed, walked softly into the living room and sat down on the couch with his feet up on the coffee table. He was thinking intently, sorting out the pattern. Demi came out a half hour later, supple, fair, and slitty-eyed again. She was wearing one of his shirts as an abbreviated nightgown. She squatted on the floor on the far side of the coffee table and looked up at him.

"I love you," she whispered. "I love you, I love you, I love you."

After a long pause he drew a shuddering breath. "You're Titanian." It was not a question.

She took a pause as long as his, then nodded. "Will it make any difference?"

"I don't know. I— You're the first I've ever met."

"In bed?"

"Anywhere."

"Are you sure?"

"N-no. I suppose I can't be. Nobody can."

"No."

"Can you be sure?"

"You mean are there mysterious clues, like secret Masonic signals? No, but—"

"But what?"

"But we *can* spot each other if we happen to speak Titanian."

"What does Titanian sound like? Have I ever heard it?"

"Maybe. This is tricky. You see, Titanians don't communicate the way the rest of the Solar does."

"No?"

"Not with sound or sight."

"How then? ESP?"

"No, we speak chemical."

"What?"

"Ours is a chemical language; scents and tastes and sensations on the skin or inside the body."

"You're zigging me on."

"Not at all. It's a highly sophisticated language of mixtures and intensity modulations."

"I don't believe it."

"You can't because it's alien to you. Here, I'll speak chemical. Ready to receive?"

"Go ahead."

After a few moments of dead silence, Demi asked, "Well?"

"Nothing."

"Smell anything? Taste anything? Feel anything?"

"Nothing."

"Receive any output of any kind at all?"

"Only the conviction that this is a con scam which— No. Wait. I have to be honest. For a moment I thought I was seeing a sort of sunburst, like these scars on my cheeks."

She beamed. "There! See? You *were* receiving me, only it's so alien to you that your mind had to translate the input into familiar symbols."

"You were actually telling me something that I translated into a visual sunburst?"

She nodded.

"What were you saying in chemical?"

"That you're a crazy, mixed-up Maori macho, and I adore every part of you, including the scars."

"You said all that?"

"And meant it, especially the scars. You're so ashamed of them, poor dear . . . "

"Don't feel sorry for me; I hate that," he growled, then, "Do you Titanians walk around, broadcasting in chemical?"

"No."

"Are there many of you here?"

"I don't know and I don't care. I only care about you . . . and you're frightening me, Rogue."

"I don't mean to."

"You're so cold and analytic after . . . after you know what."

"Forgive me." He managed a smile. "I'm trying to sort it out."

"I should never have told you."

"You didn't have to tell me; you showed me. The most extraordinary experience I ever— How do you come to be on Terra?"

"I was born here. I'm a changeling."

"What? How?"

"My real mother was a close friend of the Jeroux family. She was their doctor. I can't go into her history; it'd take ages."

"All right."

"I was a month old when their first baby died of crib-death. She substituted me for the body."

"Why on earth?"

"Because she loved them and knew the shock of losing their first child would cripple them forever. I wasn't her first . . . we shell them out rapid-fire like peas . . . "

"Your father was Terran?"

"No. We're fertile only with Titanians. Seems like our eggs don't love your sperms, or maybe vice versa. Anyway, she thought it would advantage me to be raised as a Terran in a fine family. She could always keep a Titanian eye on me, which she did. The end."

"Then you people *can* love."

"You ought to know, Rogue."

"But I don't know." He waved a helpless hand. "All that talk about Prisma hair dye and practicing eye-bits and— That was Titanian camouflage, wasn't it?"

"Yes. I try to be what you want, but my love isn't camouflage."

"And you can change yourself?"

"Yes."

"But what are you really like?"

"What do you think Titanians are really like?"

"Damn if I know." His glance to her was perplexed. "I suppose like—like a ball of burning energy or maybe a kind of plastic amoeba or maybe a bolt of lightning, eh?"

She burst out laughing. "No wonder you're

worried. Who'd want to be kissed by a thousand
volts? Tell me what *you're* really like."

"You can see for yourself, and you can believe
what you see."

"Au contraire, m'sieur," she smiled. "I won't see
what you're really like until you're dead."

"That's preposterous, Demi."

"Not at all." She became grave. "What's the real
you, the you that I love? Your genius for patterns?
Your brilliance as a synergic inquisitor? Your
wit? Your charm? Your sophistication? No. The
reality of you lies in what you *do* with all your
marvelous qualities . . . everything you contribute
and leave behind you, and we won't know that
until you're dead and gone."

"I suppose you're right," he admitted.

"And it's the same with us. Yes, I can adapt and
change to fit occasions or suit people, but not *any*
situation or *any* person. The real me is what I
chose to do. And when I die I'll look like what my
deep inside has always chosen. That'll be the real
me."

"Aren't you going mystic?"

"Not at all." She tapped the coffee table, much
in the manner of a schoolmarm illustrating a
lecture. The table was a magnificent cross section
cut from a tulip tree on Saturn VI. "Look at these
rings. Each shows a change, an adaptation, yes?"

He nodded.

"But it's still a tulip tree, yes?"

"Yes."

"It started as a tender bud which could have
grown into anything, but the Cosmic Spirit said to

it, '*You* are a tulip tree. Change and adapt as you must, but you will live and die a tulip tree.' Well, with us it's the same thing. We change and adapt, but always within the limits of what we really are deep inside."

All Winter could do was shake his head in bewilderment.

"We're polymorphs, yes," she continued, "but we live, adapt, fight to survive, fall in love—"

"And play fun love-games with us," he broke in.

"And why not? Isn't love fun?" She glared at him. "What the hell's the matter with you, Winter? D'you think love should be deep, dark, gloomy, despairing, like one of those old Russian plays? I didn't think you were that juvenile."

After a startled moment he began to shake with laughter at her outburst. "Damn you, Demi! You've adapted again. But how in God's name did you know I needed a mentor?"

She laughed with him. "I don't know, darling. Maybe with my left eye. Half the time I'm only sensing what's needed. After all, I'm only demi-human, and this is the first time I've ever been in love, so I'm not accountable."

"Never, never change," he smiled. Then, "But what the hell am I saying?"

"That I should only change for you." She took his hand. "Come on, Starstud."

o   o   o

This time they returned to the living room together. This time she sat on the couch with her feet up. She hadn't bothered with the makeshift nightgown, and now she looked like a schoolgirl athlete. "Captain of the field hockey team," Winter thought as he cross-legged on the floor across from her and admired her. She patted the cushions.

"Come sit close, darling."

"Not now. That couch talks too damn much."

"*Talks* too much?"

He nodded.

"You can't be serious, Rogue."

"Sure I am. Everything talks to me, but right now I just want to listen to you."

"Everything?"

"Uh-huh. Furniture, pictures, machines, plants, flowers . . . you name it, I hear it, when I bother to listen."

"What does the couch sound like?"

"Like . . . Mostly like a slow-motion walrus with a mouth full of cotton. Bloo—foo—goo—moo—noo— You have to be patient and listen long."

"And flowers?"

"You'd think they were skittish like giggly girls, but they're not. They're sinuous and sultry like commercials for perfumes named *C'est la Séductrice.*"

"You're on speaking terms with the whole universe," she laughed. "I think that's why I fell for you." She looked down at him. "Does anything say, 'I love you'?"

"They don't think in those terms. Egomaniacs, all of them."

"I do. I. Love. You."

His glance returned her look. "I can do better than that. I trust you."

"Why is that better?"

"Because now I can confide in you. I've got some thinking to do with you."

"You're always thinking."

"It's my one vice. Listen, love, something happened to me . . . something bad."

"Tonight?"

"On Venucci. Now you're not to repeat what I'm going to tell you to anyone. I know I can count on you for that, but you're just a kid from Virginia, even though you're Titanian, and you may be swindled into revealing something."

"I'll never reveal anything." Suddenly the captain of the field hockey team began to resemble Morgan le Fay.

"Avaunt!" he cried and crossed his arms before his face.

"Caught in the act." The sorceress grinned and transformed into the fiery Sierra O'Nolan.

"Not her!" Winter cried, remembering screaming brawls. "For God's sake, Demi . . . " And then, as she dropped the role, he grumbled, "So you Titanians aren't infallible after all."

"Of course not. Who is?" she said composedly. "And will you please stop using 'you Titanians.' It's not 'you' and 'us.' We're all part of the same joke in the Cosmic caper."

He nodded. "But sweetheart, you have to understand how tough it is to cope with mercurial love."

"Oh is it? Look, Rogue, have you ever made a connection with an actress in your raunchy

private life?" She began to resemble Sarah Bern-
hardt.

"Alas! Yes."

"And how many roles did she play, onstage and
off?"

"A jillion, maybe."

"So with us it's the same damn thing."

"But you change physically."

"Isn't makeup the same damn thing?"

"You got me, you got me," he surrendered. "I
guess I'll never know who I'm in love with. Who?
Whom? I busted grammar at the *Höhere Schule*,"
he confessed, "owing to a surfeit of adverbs."

"You *are* a genius," she crinkled, "and I'm going
to learn from you."

"I'm afraid I'm a father image for you."

"Then we've been incestuous."

"Well, I've broken most of the Ten Commandments, so what's another? Brandy?"

"Perhaps later, please."

Winter got a bottle of cognac and two claret
glasses, put the stemware down on the coffee
table, opened the bottle and had a belt from it.
"I've broken another."

"Which?"

"Isn't Marymount a Catholic-type college?"

"More or less."

"Did *les Jeroux* raise their changeling kid a
Catholic?"

"More or less."

"Then this may shock you. The sixth."

"Thou shalt not—? No!"

"Uh-huh."

"You're trying out a story on me."

Winter shook his head. "It happened in the Bologna Dome, my last day there."

"But— But—" She leaped up, looking like one of the avenging Furies, and Winter imagined he could see serpents twined in her hair. "Rogue Winter, if you're zigging me on, I'll—"

"No, no, no," he interrupted. "Would I joke about a thing like that, Demi?"

"Yes you would. You're a wicked liar."

He patted the couch. "Sit down, love. It's a story all right, but I didn't invent it. It happened, and I have to talk it over with someone I can trust."

She sat down, still suspicious. "So? Tell."

"I came across the tail end of a peculiar pattern in Bologna which involved the Meta Mafia. You know the Triton Jinks have a lock on Meta, and they're tough. They set prices and quotas, and if they don't like the Inner Barbarians for any reason, they cut your quota. So naturally there's a Meta Mafia smuggling the stuff out of Triton. Their prices are outlandish but they deliver, no matter who or what you are. Sort of nice-guy goniffs. Clear so far?"

"Except Meta," she said slowly. "I know it stands for metastasis, which produces energy, but how?"

"It's kind of complicated."

"I'll try."

"Well, start with atoms and charged particles. They can be kicked from their normal state into an excited state by Meta. This absorbs energy from the Meta. Then they flop back into their normal state, releasing that energy, and that's the metastasic process. Dig?"

"No. Too scientific, and I'm not going to try to look like Marie Curie."

"She was no looker anyway. All right. You tried talking chemical to me; I'll try talking pattern to you. I want you to think of a laser beam that can drill a hole through steel or carry a message across space . . . "

"Got that?"

"No pattern yet. Just a straight line."

"Ah, but how's that line produced? Think of a cloud of particles in their normal rest state . . . sort of like a gang of zeros . . . "

```
          o  o
         o  o  o
       o  o  o  o  o
         o  o  o  o
     o  o  o  o  o  o  o
       o  o  o  o  o
         o  o  o  o  o
           o  o  o
```

"Now we stimulate this crowd into an excited state by pouring energy into them. That kicks them up into particles-plus . . . "

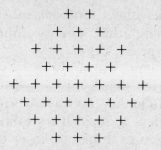

"But this isn't a natural stable condition, it's a
sort of nuclear hysteria, and they start to quit and
go back to their normal, comfortable zero rocking
chairs . . . Got the pattern?"

"*Continuez. Continuez lentement.*"

"They're not freeloaders, so a particle gives up
the energy it's received, which coaxes a couple
more of its chums back into their normal rest
state, giving up *their* energy, which cues four
more, and then eight take the hint, and sixteen,
thirty-two, sixty-four, and it builds until you've
got all that energy emerging as a beam."

```
            o  +
         o  o  +    +
      +     +     +     +
      +  o     +   +
   o o    +  o + + +  +
 +  +  +++++++++++++++
    +  o   +  +++
      +   +   +  +
         +  +
```

"All in nanoseconds and all in phase, which is

what gives it its power. Got the picture?"

"Yes, but where does Meta come in?"

"Well, it takes a tremendous amount of energy to stimulate atoms and particles into the excited state, more than they give back; so when you balance profit and loss, you wind up in the red. But when you use Meta to excite them, you're in the black. You spend one and get back a hundred."

"Why? How?"

"Because that freak catalyst is a powerhouse of stored energy fighting to get out. There's stored energy in everything, Demi, and all it needs is an electron transfer system to be released. Think of a match. You've got a chemical head of potash, antimony, and stuff, full of energy waiting to be released. Friction does it. But when Meta excites and releases energy, it's like a stick of dynamite compared to a match. It's the chess legend for real."

"I don't know it."

"Oh, the story goes that a philosopher invented chess for the amusement of an Indian rajah. The king was so delighted that he told the inventor to name his reward and he'd get it, no matter what. The philosopher asked that one grain of rice be placed on the first square of the chessboard, two on the second, four on the third, and so on to the sixty-fourth."

"That doesn't sound like much."

"So the rajah said. He'd expected a request for gold and jewels and stuff. This, he thought, was too modest until he discovered that all the rice in India and China wouldn't be enough to fill that last square. That's geometric progression for you, and it's what Meta does for energy."

"How did it get that way?"

"I don't know. I've always wanted to do a full feature on it but never could get started because the Jinks on Triton refused to cooperate. The only thing our local physicists can tell me is that it reverses entropy, and good luck to them."

"What's entropy?"

"Didn't they learn you nothing in that high-class collitch you took from?"

"The foreign-language department didn't offer any courses in entropy."

"It's not a language, it's Decadence 101. Entropy is decay. If you leave a physical system alone, its entropy increases, which means that it runs down and flakes out and its energy available for work peters out too. The stored power in Meta reverses that with one hell of a shot in the arm."

"Zig wow! It *is* complicated."

"Yeah, it's a race apart."

"What does Meta look like?"

"I've never seen it. The engineers protect it like eunuchs defending a harem. No visitors. No sight-seeing. They say it's too dangerous— Stop that, Demi!— I can't say I blame them. There's been too many damnfool accidents in the past."

Demi abandoned her transformation into a naked concubine and said, "Now go on about the Sixth Commandment."

"Now?"

"Please."

"But I want to talk about the wonderful thing that's happened between us."

"Later."

"It may be too late. *Love is not a faucet,*" he sang, miserably. *"It don't turn off and on . . . "*

"Yes, your voice is beautifully entropic, in four flats. Now what about the Sixth Commandment? Please, Rogue, it's blocking what's between us."

"It is?"

She nodded. "I can feel it when you love me . . . a tiny thundercloud hanging over you . . . "

"My God," he whispered, half to himself, "you're fantastic . . . To sense that . . . even while you were ravishing me . . . "

"Please, darling, be serious."

"Just trying to shift gears," he said uncomfortably. "Give me a moment."

Demi lapsed into a sympathetic silence. He drummed his fingers softly, staring into the past, and once murmuring, "Don't bother me now," to whichever picture or piece of furniture that was intruding with a subsonic soliloquy. At last he looked at Demi.

"You know that Venucci isn't exclusively Italian," he began. "It's more Mediterranean; Greek, Portuguese, Algerian, Albanian, and so on. They all cling to their own traditions and life-styles, and the Italian Domes hold on to regional cultures and local subcultures, too; Sicilian, Neapolitan, Venetian, and even New York Little Italy. They speak Slum-Italo-English and the Saint's Day festivals in the Mulberry Dome are a riot."

She nodded again, still silent, wondering where he was headed.

His quick eye caught her expression and he smiled. "Wait for it. Wait for it. Once a Soup-Kwik company asked me why Bologna was the only Italian Dome that would buy their product. I had to explain that Italian wives were traditional home-bodies who took pride in preparing their own soups. The Bolognese were the exception because their women preferred careers, you know, down with *Kinder, Kirche und Küche,* and they all came home and slapped packaged dinners together."

"I'm with them."

"I'm not against. Bologna is the hot center of the Women's Movement on Venucci. Most of their *polizia* are women; big, tough ginzo dykes you wouldn't want to mess around with, but there was one remarkable exception, a delicate little thing and—here it comes—she was a Jink."

"What? On Venucci?"

"In the Bologna Dome, and that gave me furiously to synergize, particularly because she was in heavy money—expensive tailored uniforms, posh restaurants, luxury transport, that sort of thing—so you can guess what I was synsensing."

"She was a Mafia rep."

"And a possible lead to their operation on Triton, which was a pattern I'd been yearning to expose. I didn't sense that this was the wrong end. I turned on the charm and finally dated her to meet me in the central gardens when she came off duty. That was my last night in the Bologna Dome."

"And you killed her?" Demi was horrified.

"I got there early to case the gardens—it's a wild playground for Lib women cruising for studs; dark, misty, shadowy—and on the very spot where she'd promised to meet, this gorill came crashing out of the bushes and hit me with everything he had."

"Holy bolido! And . . . ?"

"And I broke the Sixth."

"But— But how?"

"Demi, I'm not going into details, but if there's one thing the Maori hammer into a future king, it's how to defend and kill in hand-to-hand."

"Who was he? I mean, could it have been a mistake?"

"It wasn't any mistake, and that's why I'm having fantods . . . because he was carrying a Slice Knife—that's a kind of knife the Maori use to cut out the heart of a brave enemy to eat for its courage—"

"Ugh!"

"Yes, and his I.D. papers read: Kea Ora—Ganymede. He was a Maori killer."

"My God! My God! And did the Mafia girl come?"

"I didn't wait to find out. I took the knife, left the bod under a bush, and got lost. So now you can understand what's zigging me into zags. Look at it. Had I slipped and given the Jink a clue to what I was really after? Did her Mafia turn me over to a hit man? And why pick a Maori soldier, one of my own people, and what the hell was he doing on Venucci anyway? Will their *polizia* find out that I'm the alleged perpetrator and will they come after me? Does the Mafia still have a contract out on me? *Oi veh! Shlog'n kop in vant!*"

After she'd taken in as much of Winter's head-banging as she could absorb, Demi asked, "You have that Maori Slice Knife?"

"Still in my travel tote."

"May I see it, please?"

He brought the knife and she examined it cautiously. It looked like a pointed straight razor, hollow-ground, glittering and deadly. There was no guard. The handle was natural walnut, much worn from long use, blotched with red smudges.

"I killed him with it. That's why I had to take it. Prints."

"So it's true, what you told me." She put the knife down very carefully.

"All of it."

"I think I need that brandy now, please."

He filled both claret glasses and they drank together in a long, silent meditation. Then the cognac seemed to restore his poise. "Cheer up, love," he grinned. "I'll come out of this smelling like roses. You'll see."

"Please make that 'we'll.' I want to be in it with you," she said earnestly.

"Thank you. Instant dumb loyalty. You're a right Titanian tootsie."

She had to laugh. "Damn you, Winter! You'll joke in your coffin. What fantastic things happen to you. I wonder why."

He refilled their glasses. "I don't know. Maybe because I invite them without meaning to. After all, you're a fantastic thing that's happened to me, and I swear I never invited it."

She finished her cognac and announced, "I'm going to make a confession," beginning to look like Saint Joan of Arc. "It wasn't any accident. When I realized I wanted you, I set out to get you. I looked up everything about you, talked to people who knew you, spent days going through everything you ever wrote . . . . You didn't stand a chance. Don't hold it against me."

"Your halo's showing," he murmured.

She slopped another cognac into her glass. "Why did you say you needed a girl?" she demanded. "You must have hundreds."

"No."

"How many?"

"You ask the damnedest questions. What's Demi short for, Demon?"

"Neh-neh-neh-neh-NO. Fifth Amendment."

"Now, Demi . . ."

"Never."

"One call to payroll and you're doomed."

"You wouldn't!"

"I have you in my power."

"You won't hold it against me?"

"Second Amendment."

"What's that?"

"Right to bear arms."

"Well . . . I told you I was raised down south. Typical fine Virginia family, so I'm a typical fine Virginia girl . . ." She gulped. "W-with a typical fine Virginia name."

"Consisting of?"

"Demure," she whispered.

"What!" He began to break up.

She responded with hauteur. "My full name, suh, is Demure Recamier Jeroux, and ah *defies* y'all."

"Why Recamier?" he asked faintly.

"Madame Recamier is mama's hero."

"I see. Now listen, my stoned sprite, you've got a kid's idea that I'm a Casanova with like a Women's Corps at my beck and call. That just isn't true of myself or any man. Women are always in control and they make the decisions."

"Saying that I seduced you. I knew you'd hold it against me."

"Damn right you did. So now you've had your Titanian will of me, what?"

"I still want to know why you said you needed a girl when I made my move in the conference room."

He took a long beat, then, "Isn't it obvious? I'm not always jaunty-jolly under the gun. 'Damn the torpedoes, full speed ahead.' 'You may fire when ready, Gridley.' There come times when I lose my cool and I'm upset and confused and frightened like I am now. Then every instinct makes me turn to a woman for comfort and support."

"Ssss."

"What are you sissing about?"

"Because I'm your mother image," she said with delight. "It's double incest."

"All you southerin types love decadence. Or is it the Titanian in you?"

"I was pure, sir, until I was *dépravée* by a surfeit of Maori."

"How dast you steal my type line?"

She put her glass down firmly. "What time is it?"

"Fourish."

"I've got to get dressed."

"What's the rush? Where are you going?"

"Home, silly." She arose from the couch. "I've got to change to block gossip at the office. There'll be scam enough as it is. And I have to feed my cat."

"Cat!" he exclaimed. "A fine Virginia girl like you wasting herself on a cat?"

"She's special. She chases the spots you see before your eyes. She's a psycat and I love her."

"I will be damned. I'll see you home, of course."

"Thank you. What are *we* going to do about your problems?"

"Cool it and wait for the next move."

"Are you in any danger?" she asked anxiously.

"Not really." He looked up at her with love, pulled her close and nuzzled her belly.

"No fair," she giggled. "You're tickling. Get up, Starpooped. Let's get dressed."

"You meant that to sting."

"Yes, now that I've robbed you of your manhood I've no more use for you. That's the Titanian way."

o   o   o

"I'm bowlegged," she called from her dressing room, not complaining. "Are you always so passionate?"

"Only the first time around. Showing off. We all do that."

"I'll make sure it's always the first time around with us." She poked her head out. "Why aren't you exhausted, too?"

"I don't know. Maybe it's because I've stolen your Titanian essence. Rogue, the Vampire, they call me."

"Why on earth are you blinking like that?"

"Trying to work up spots before my eyes for your alleged psycat to chase." He fondled the pet which was an affectionate Saturnian crossbreed, an odd blending of Siamese with koala. "She *is* a beauty. Does she chase her own spots?"

"But of course; all cats do. I've finished changing now. Time to go."

"I'll walk you to the office."

"Only as far as the corner, I beg. If we're seen together at the main entrance first thing in the morning . . . Well! Do I call you or you me?"

"You call me, and for God's sake use your own Virginia voice. Don't spring like a Mata Hari on me."

"C'est magnifique," she answered in throbbing spy-sultry tones, *"mais ce n'est pas la guerre.* Come on, Starjock."

"I'll give you the plans for the secret invasion," he whined, "if you'll only let me out of your secret thrall."

Chapter Four

CORONATION

On the King's gate the moss grew gray;
   The King came not. They called him
     dead
And made his eldest son one day
   Slave in his father's stead.
                —Helen Hunt Jackson

After he'd kissed Demi (out of sight of gossip) Winter continued on foot toward the *Beaux Arts* rotunda. It was a brilliant morning in classy New York, the Jungle-Mother, and the entire Wasp world seemed to reflect his own exhilaration. Anachronistic Christmas displays in shop windows: *!!It's Xmas On Mars!!Send A Gift To Your Loved One!!* Porno Valentine decorations posted by striking hookers seeking support. White linens hanging from windowsills to demonstrate sympathy with the Honk Movement fighting for a Dome on Ganymede.

Some sort of advertising parade came down the main stem; a fife-and-drum corps with almost as many twirlers as drummers, making a hell of a racket which was compounded by a street gang of young hoods, "Titan Dukes" their jackets proclaimed in neon, leaping and cavorting in ludicrous passes at the twirlers. Then came the hard-sell float for $P+L+A+Z+M+I+L+K$ with eight farm girls (live) milking eight Holsteins (plastic).

The Synergist stopped dead in his tracks, as

though paralyzed by a mysterious laser pistol yet to be invented. "Eight!" he exclaimed. He turned, ran, and caught up with the head of the parade and counted the drummers. "Yes, twelve." He counted the Titan Dukes, the fifes, the twirlers. "Eleven, ten, nine, by God! Jigjeeze!"

He resumed his walk toward the rotunda, every synergic perception prickling and exploring. He spotted more of the pattern, a toy shop at the entrance to an arcade. There was a magnificent dollhouse displayed in the window. It was set in a miniature park built to scale. On a tiny pond floated seven swans. Winter nodded and entered the arcade. He was not surprised to be led around a corner by a gourmet shop which had six Canadas lying on crushed ice in the vitrine.

"Gig," he murmured. "Dukes are lords. Canadas are geese. What next?"

All thought of getting back to the rotunda had left him. He explored, sensing, searching, until he found it at last at the foot of a flight of stone steps, a poster for some flower show decorated with a stylized Gold-poppy made up of four rings for the petals and a center ring for the carpel.

"Uh-huh. Five gold rings."

He mounted the stairs, came into another arcade, passed a pet shop with a window full of puppies, continued, then stopped and shook his head. "Starschmuck!" he muttered and returned to the pet shop. He peered in. At last he saw it. a large cage at the far end. It contained four myna birds. He went in for a closer look.

"Do they talk?" he asked the owner.

"Can't shut 'em up. Only trouble is, they holler in Gullah. That's why the price is so cheap."

"It figures. Thanks."

Winter went out the back door, wondering how three French hens would be made manifest. It was managed by a blackboard in front of a restaurant. On it was chalked:

TODAY'S MENU

Poulet Gras Poularde
Poulet de l'Année
Vieille Poule Coq
      w. Sauce Indienne
      or Sauce Paprika
      or Sauce Estragon
Burgundy, Bordeaux, Côtes du Rhône

Before Winter could enter in search of two turtledoves, two young ladies came out. They were dressed in the latest trendy high style, including enormous *Eugénie* hats. Each had a tiny red jeweled-quail perched on the brim.

"*Natürlich,*" Winter said to himself. "Ruddy quail. A form of turtledove. Two."

He followed the young ladies at a discreet distance, now searching right and left for some kind of tree. There are no trees in that section of the Mighty Metrop., but the ladies entered a towering office building. Above the cathedral entrance was graven in English Gothic: PAIRE BANQUE ALSACIENNE BLDG. Winter began to chuckle. The pattern had turned into a preposterous treasure hunt, and he was wondering what absurd prize he would find at the end.

He went in, crossed directly to the tenant listings and didn't waste any time; merely glanced at "P," found "Odessa Partridge—3030" took the express elevator to the thirtieth floor, and there it was, an impressive tree-paneled door labeled PARTRIDGE. Winter entered.

He found himself in what appeared to be a full symphony orchestra waiting for the musicians to appear. He was surrounded by every known instrument; strings, brass, woodwinds, percussion. A charming young lady, no longer wearing a *Eugénie* hat, approached and greeted him. "Good morning, Mr. Winter. So glad you could keep your appointment. The spinet is ready for inspection. Frances!"

"Spinet?" Winter echoed feebly.

"Well, really, a virginal. You know, a lap-spinet without legs. Frances, please take Mr. Winter to the studio."

A second charming young lady, also without hat, had appeared and now conducted Winter through the orchestra. "We had trouble bringing it up to concert pitch," she confided. "I do hope you're not fussy about a 439 A, Mr. Winter. 435 is the most the strings would hold. In here, Mr. Winter." She opened the studio door and the bewildered Winter was gently urged in.

"Good morning, King R-og," I said.

I didn't think he heard me. He just stared, then. "But you're the nice lady from Dr. Yael's talk-in. The diva lady. I thought you should sing Brünnehilde."

"You never told me," I said. "I'm Odessa Partridge. In the music trade but not a singer."

He looked around with his quick eyes; at the thick insulated walls, the double-glazed windows, the stacked music in print and manuscript, the gilt harpsichord, the virginal, the concert grand piano with Jay Yael seated at it, smiling benignly.

"And Dr. Yael?"

"Good morning, son."

"This is too much for me."

"No, it isn't boy. Sit down. I've never seen you lose your poise for more than a moment. You'll regroup."

Winter backed into a chair and sat, shaking his head. Then drew a deep breath, compressed his lips and looked hard at me. "And this is the prize at the end of the treasure hunt?"

"There! You see?" Yael beamed. "It didn't take you five seconds, Rogue."

"But why this ridiculous Roguemarole?"

"We had to brief you on something extremely sensitive," I told him.

"So? Couldn't you call?"

"I said 'sensitive.' Calls can be tapped. And messages. And word of mouth. The problem was how to bring you here without a clue to anyone, so we relied on your pattern sense, which is unique. No one else has that."

"Forgive me, Brünnehilde, but you're sounding like an X-rated spy feature."

"We had all last night when you were—otherwise occupied, to set up 'The Twelve Days of Christmas.'"

"Naturally, your name being Partridge. But if

it'd been Kallikak?"

"I knew you'd be the only one able to sense the pattern, and if you were tailed, your course would be so eccentric that you'd certainly shake it."

"Tailed? Oh sure. Rogue Moriarty, they call me," Winter laughed. "Paging Sherlock Holmes."

"This is serious, son," Yael said.

"Why *King* R-og?" Winter shot at me.

"You're brilliant," I said with genuine admiration. "Because that's the crux and you've synergized it already. Te Uinta's soul now resides in your left eye."

"When? How?" Like lightning.

"A week ago. Hunting accident. His suit ripped open by a tusk. He was really too old to encounter an anaerobic mammoth alone."

Winter swallowed hard. "He had to prove himself. Once a year. It's the Maori tradition for royalty."

"And now you'll have to," I said. "Please listen, Winter, and don't zag in. Gig?"

He nodded.

"We've been using you, without your knowledge, for years and you've been invaluable. You've been watched and followed. Your code I.D. is 'Pointer.'" And I told him about our Pert operations and the unconscious role he played in them. He listened intently without interupting. He was quick and perceptive and didn't plague me with obvious questions like who "we" were. Once, however, he did dart a glance at Yael, who responded with a shrug.

"Now the crux," I went on. "That soldier in the

Bologna gardens carried a Slice Knife for two purposes. One was for the kill, of course, but the other was to bring your cheeks back to Ganymede."

"Ah!"

"Yes. He had nothing to do with the Jink girl from Triton or her organization. He was only stalking you as R-og Uinta, king-presumptive."

"So!"

"So indeed. There's a small, tough terrorist group who don't want you. You're not a Maori. You weren't raised in the Dome. You're Honk-corrupted. You're soft. You can't be trusted. Etcetera. Etcetera. What's their answer? Wipe you, and they're on the wipe. These killers are trained and smart, and that's why I had to go through the 'Twelve Days' caper to bring you here."

"They're wasting their time," Winter said. "I don't want any part of the king-bit."

"That won't make any difference to them. No matter who they acclaim in your place, you'll always be a present danger. The majority in the Dome will forever homage your cheeks. Their only answer is to bring your cheeks home as trophies of the kill."

"I'll abdicate formally."

"It won't go down with them. They won't trust you to stay abdicted. They'll stay on the wipe until you're blown."

"Jigjeeze! What a hell of a scam for a nice goyisha boychick. And now that Demi and I—" He cut himself off. Then; "But you didn't paper-chase me here just to bring the bad news from Ganymede to Terra. You have something more in mind. What?"

"Go to Ganymede and get yourself kinged."

"You've got to be zigging."

"Yael will accompany you."

"What's the doctor got to do with this?"

"I've never told you, son, but Te Uinta paid for your upbringing and education. He believed it could advantage the Maori to be led by a king who was conversant with our ways."

"Yes, yes," Winter muttered. "Same like Demi's Titanian mother."

"And I owe it to Te to see you through this *crise*," Yael continued. "I must; otherwise all our prep. will go down the drain."

"It's down already, sir. I'm not the king type and never will be."

"But you'll be alive," I said. "They won't dare hit you once you're formally coronated. That would alienate them from the majority completely."

"What in hell are you trying to do, Odessa, protect me? I can protect myself, now that I've been alerted. God knows, I proved that on Venucci."

"I'm not protecting *you*," I flared. "I'm protecting the *job* you're doing for us. If you have to live on the alert for hits, you won't be any use to us. The only patterns you'll be able to sense will be potential wipes."

He grunted.

"But if you get yourself coronated, you'll be safe, back to normal, business as usual." I let that sink in, then, "And your girl will be safe, too."

He glared at me. "You bitch," he said softly.
"You unadulterated, natural, organic bitch. You
know how to twist a man, don't you?"

"That's my business."

"Yeh. Like music. 'Music of the Fears.' Demi
will have to be protected while I'm gone."

"I'll take care of that."

"Gig. When?"

I liked him even more for that. Once he'd made a
decision, he was ready to act without any fuss.
"Noon jet today. Yael's made all the arrange-
ments."

"That vig, huh?"

"Best and safest."

"And you knew you had my number. You'll explain to Demi after I leave?"

"As much as is good for her to know. Trust me."

"I have to. *Avanti, dottore!*" Winter was on his
feet moving fast. "Did I ever tell you the one about
the mammoth that robbed the jewelry store?"

o   o   o

With the aid and comfort of Meta power, jet
travel is a matter of days and weeks which gives
the Jap-Chinks yet another stranglehold. It's the
price the Solar must pay for its transformation
from isolated outposts into a close community of
quarreling planets and satellites, and another
torque which turns the Meta Mafia into bootlegging Good Guys. (At a conservative estimate,
some 5,271,009 hours have been devoted to

researching an analysis and synthesis of Meta. No way, but not to contemn; the ancients put in as much time chasing the Philosopher's Stone.)

Winter and Yael arrived at the main lock of the Maori Dome via terrafoil (Ganyfoil?). It was the second of the three days of direct sunlight and it was reasonably bright and pleasant. If the interior of the Dome resembles anything it's Rapa Nui, i.e. "Great Rapa," otherwise known as Easter Island.

There are differences, to be sure. It's circular rather than triangular. No thatched huts; the little houses are drywall. No giant stone images; instead, huge carved tribal totems (with left eyes of inlaid mica) before each family of houses. All delightfully primitive, but the central kampong in which the Maori assemble to exercise, compete, quarrel, gossip, ceremonize, u.s.w., covers the ultramodern Dome maintenance system which, after the JonesDome disaster on Mercury, is Death City taboo for any except authorized technicians to enter.

Yael had been invaluable on the outjet. He dyed Winter with a sepiawood to conform to the Maori brown skin, this over Winter's bitter objections. (It's believed that woad induces impotence.) "Public relations, son. The impotence has never been verified, and anyway the dye will be worn out by the time you get back to your woman."

"And so will I, from worrying."

"Just worry about the mammoth."

They passed through the lock and entered the Dome, expecting pandemonium—Yael had lasered advance notice of their arrival—but were met with solemn ritual. The twelve tribal chiefs, feathered, pearled, necklaced, braceleted and ankleted, were in a semicircle. They genuflected, advanced, and gently stripped Winter naked.

"Oparo? Is that you?" Winter stammered, half in Polynesian, half in English. "I've been gone so long. Tubuai? We used to wrestle; you always beat me. Waihu? Remember the time we tried to climb your totem and got walloped? Teapi? Chincha?" No answer.

There had never been a coronation in Winter's lifetime so he didn't know what to expect, but he discovered that all his anticipations had been wrong. No frantic mobs, no cheers, no drums, no song; instead he was escorted, stark naked, across the deserted kampong in stately silence and reverently desposited alone in the Te Uinta palace which he remembered so well.

It was enormous by Maori standards, ten separate rooms, now all bare. The house had been stripped of everything; it was merely four walls. Winter squatted in the center of the main hall, which had been as much of a throne room as the Maori cared for, and waited for the next move. There was none. He waited, waited, waited.

"I wonder if the doctor is getting the same treatment," he wondered, stretching out on the floor.

(Yael was being lavishly entertained. They remembered him with affection.)

"I suppose I'm supposed to be in solemn meditation," Winter meditated. "The awesome responsibilities facing me. What I owe to my ancestors and my people. So. On my honor I will do my best to do my duty to God and my country and to obey the Scout Law . . .

"And this guy came to his jewelry store early one morning to catch up with his paper work. He got there just in time to see a truck back up to his store. The rear opened and this hairy mammoth got out, went to the store window, smashed it with his tusks, and scooped up all the goodies with his trunk. Then he got back into the truck and it drove away . . ."

There was a rustling and a chiming. Winter looked toward the sound and discovered that a brown girl had crept into the room. She had the typical black wavy hair—the Maori are either straight or wavy, never curly—attractive Polynesian features and an adolescent body. He could see that because she wore a chain of chiming silver scallops around her waist and nothing else.

"What the hell is this?" he asked himself. "Part of the ritual? My future consort and queen? They ought to let me choose for myself."

The girl wasted no time. She was against him in a moment, silently entwining and exciting, and it seemed to him that she was giving one hell of an audition for the consort role until he felt the initial slash against the back of his knee. His trained reflexes were like lightning. He drove the knee up into her crotch and smashed the razor-edged shell out of her hand. As she doubled over in agony he muttered, "The hamstring-bit, huh? Odessa was right. These cats are no clowns. The mammoth hunt would've been real jaunty-jolly with me hamstrung."

He picked the helpless girl up and gave himself the satisfaction of biting her rump hard enough to draw blood before he threw her out the front door like a piece of trash. Then he slammed the door to give notice that he'd take on anything, and settled down again on the throne-room floor, alert for further action. He didn't yet realize that the attack and his response was reverting him to the sanguinary for which the future king had been trained.

After a half hour of quiet, he resumed his customary internal discourse. "So, as I was saying when I was so rudely interrupted: this guy watches the truck drive off, absolutely flabbergasted, and finally pulls himself together and calls the cops. They come, he tells, and they're very professional. 'We have to have some kind of lead. Did you dig the license number?' 'No. All I saw was that hairy elephant.' 'What kind of truck was it?' 'I don't know. All I could look at was that goddam mammoth.' 'All right, what kind of mammoth was it?' 'You mean there's different kinds?' 'Why yes. The Asian mammoth has big floppy ears. The American mammoth has small, tight ears. Which kind did this one have?'"

He fell asleep on that question.

He was awakened by a tumult. He scrambled to his feet, opened the palace door and looked out. The kampong was jammed with Maori; shouting, singing, stamping, pounding drums. The twelve tribal chiefs were advancing, carrying Te Uinta's six-foot royal shield and royal spear, both of which Winter recognized instantly.

"Ears! Ears!" he muttered. "How could I tell? That goddam mammoth was wearing a stocking over his head."

That was his last clutch on Solar English. Now he was completely reverted, thinking and acting in Maori. He stepped outside the door, naked and regal, and when the delegation arrived, he touched each chieftain on the heart, murmuring the formal greeting. They shouldered the shield and he permitted himself to be raised onto it, standing tall and unafraid for all to see.

He was carried the full circuit of the kampong three times, and the excitement was deafening. The shield was lowered to the ground and still he stood, proud and expectant. A priest—actually a shaman—appeared for the unction, carrying an urn of oil. Long-buried memory stirred, and Winter knew it was the fat from his adoptive father's body. He was anointed; top of head, eyes, sunburst cheeks, breast, palms and loins.

"Now is crowned King of the Seven War Canoes," the shaman shouted. "Of Hawaiki, Apai, Evava, and Maori. R-og Uinta, son and next heir to our last king departed."

Te Uinta's diadem, a wide band of silver and jet threads, was bound around Rogue's head.

"He and no other!" the shaman challenged.

Dead silence.

The chieftains advanced and placed Te Uinta's royal fighting spear in Rogue's hand like a scepter, and there was pandemonium. Now he must go out to kill a mammoth single-handed and prove his royal right to rule.

o　　o　　o

The Ganymede mammoth is yet another example of cosmic eccentricity (Demi Jeroux prefers to call it "The Cosmic *Marâtre*") aided and abetted by Man.

One of the Solar's favorite foods (barring kinky religious sects) is pork. Now pigs are wonderful people. They're bright, active, and superbly adaptable. They really don't want to lie in a coma and stink; it's only the ones gorged on garbage and fattening in muddy styes that do. Anyone who's ever seen a clean, active sow galloping happily in a meadow, surrounded by a cluster of her playful piglets, knows that. Unhappily, when pork is bred for weight, it must wallow in mud to support its mass, and it snores and stinks to high heaven, which is how most of us see pigs.

But a Dome can't cope with animal stenches (it has enough trouble coping with people) so the breeders and butchers appealed to the genetic mavins to engineer a hog species that could survive in paddocks outside a Dome in the near-anaerobic, murderous Ganymede environment.

The genetic engineers were delighted with the odd challenge and selected the Tamworth, one of the oldest breeds of pigs, as the best candidate. The Tamworth is hardy, active and prolific, and closely related to the wild boar. The head, body, and legs are long, and the ribs deep and flat. Its disposition leaves much to be desired.

The geneticists back-bred the Tamworth; that is, reversed the development of the pig back to its wild origins by selective breeding, while they evolved its hardiness into a tolerance for anaerobic conditions, rooting for oxygen among other needs. The result was the Ganymede "Astroboar" which was raised at minimum cost and sold to the Solar at fashionable prices. It was advertised with:

DO NOT BE A PARTY-POOPER!
ASTROBOAR WILL MAKE HOSTS SOOPER!

And:

NO FATSO
NO SALTSO
NO CHOLESTER ALSO
LIVE LONGER ON THE HOG
LIVE HIGHER ON ASTROBOAR

An occasional pig would break out of a paddock and take to the rills. The breeders shrugged. It wasn't worthwhile chasing them and anyway they were bound to die, but here the Cosmic Caper took a hand. Somewhat like those first primal fish stranded on beaches by the ebbing tide and surviving nevertheless, these rare independents survived nevertheless, rooting the frozen terrain for subsoil mosses and lichens. They lived precariously, they encountered each other, they mated, many died, the most adaptable evolved into the strange breed that Ganymede calls The Mammoth.

Actually, they're more a gigantic wild boar than elephant. They can stand nearly two meters high at the shoulder, whereas the original *Mammuthus* stood closer to four. Their ears are elephantine to absorb as much sunlight as possible. They're hairy, like the woolly mammoth. Their upcurved tusks are enormous for rooting in frozen soil.

The original Tamworth breed was omnivorous and so are the Ganymede mammoths, plus the fact that survival desperation has turned them cannibal. In temperament they're pure wild boar; irascible, vicious, attacking. They reduce survival to a deadly bottom line.

This was the half-ton number that Winter had to track and kill. "And I don't even like pork," he thought.

He was in a vacsuit, helmeted, air-tanked, carrying the long-bladed hunting spear and belted with a Slice Knife to bring the heart back as a trophy, and then eat for its sympathetic magic. The Maori wanted their ruler to acquire the wild ferocity of the mammoth, which is why tradition demanded the kill once a year.

"And which is ridiculous for me," Winter argued. "I'm a sissy Solar." But he was talking to himself in Maori.

The terrain was lunar and jagged; mantle rock, shale, slate, igneous outcrops, black obsidian—a glassy souvenir of Ganymede's volcanic past—the splintered cleavages revealing the sickly white remains of mineral-anabolic fungi; one of the foods the mammoth feed on in addition to themselves. (Give life one chance in a thousand, and it will seize it and never let go.)

An hour out of the Dome, Winter came across the first mammoth sign, droppings in the form of conical pats. The mammoth feeds and excretes constantly. He followed the trail cautiously, saw it joined by others, and came at last to a shallow crater scattered with pats.

He grunted. "Mammoth kampong."

Then the hunter took over. "Mistake Te Uinta made. They all make, and get killed. You don't go in after the mammoth; you're fighting his savvy. Make him come after you and fight yours. Yes."

A glance at the sinking spotlight sun and giant limb of Jupiter on the horizon. An hour until the three-day night began. Enough time before the quasi-nocturnals came out to feed.

He backtracked, searching, and located a small crater with a ten-foot-high rim. Meteor impact, probably. The crater floor was cracked, crazed schist. He nodded, loped to the obsidian outcrop he had passed and collected long glass splinters, careful not to pierce his vacsuit. With his metal soles he kicked and shattered off even longer stalacts. These he planted in the crazed cracks of the crater floor, close to the ten-foot rim. It was a bed of spikes awaiting a fakir.

He stood erect, breathed hard, swallowed saliva and tried to fill the attached urine sac. He reached back over his shoulder and opened the tank valve to full blast until the vacsuit stretched to Santa Claus dimensions. He bent forward, dove a hand through the taped anal flap and whipped the urine sac between his legs and out. By the time he had the flap resealed and the air pressure adjusted, his urine was frozen.

Winter climbed over the ten-foot crater rim and trekked back to the mammoth kampong, dropping chips of his urine which he cracked off with the Slice Knife. The kampong was still empty, but the sun had set, the stars were brilliant, and Saturn dominated the sky, looking like a lobed light bulb, the rings not quite distinguishable to the unaided eye. Winter dumped the last of his urine, ground his soles into it, and tramped more trail back to the outer edge of the crater rim. There he waited with spear and knife.

He was forced to stand; that brief exposure had frostbitten his rump painfully.

He waited, keeping faith with the territorial challenge of alien urine.

He tested the spear shaft. It was spun glass and had the strength and resilience of a vaulting pole.

He waited.

He collected a small pile of rounded stones which would not tear his gloves.

He waited.

He waited.

A bull boar came at last, snuffling silently at the urine *défi*, icy iron hair bristling, bloody crusted eyes rolling, flap ears vibrating, giant tusks gleaming in the starlight, half a ton of mammoth menace. Winter picked up a stone, threw it hard and missed. He threw three more before he hit the beast and caught its angry attention. Winter leaped, waved, threw another stone, darted forward, shook the spear, darted back and threw still another stone which caught the mammoth full on the snout.

The beast finally made the furious connection and charged, tail up, head lowered, tusks poised to rip from crotch to neck. It took all Winter's nerve to freeze and observe the attack like a matador estimating the speed of his enemy. At the last possible moment he turned, sprinted three steps, and pole-vaulted over the crater rim to land just beyond the bed of glass spikes. He spun around on his knees. The mammoth had pursued him, scrambled over the rim, and plunged into the spike bed. It was thrashing in agony from a dozen stabs piercing the soft belly. Its blood was freezing as it poured out.

Winter got to his feet, looked for the spear, then remembered it had dropped outside the crater rim. He shuddered slightly, realizing the risk he had run. If the beast hadn't fallen onto the spikes . . . ! Anyway, there was no need to administer a finishing stroke; the mammoth would be dead in a matter of minutes.

He watched the violent death. Then his sharp vigilance was caught by flying stone fragments. He looked. It was the bull's sow, struggling over the edge of the crater rim. She had followed at a slower pace.

The sow slid down the inner wall, rolled safely against the last standing spikes, smashing them flat, and was on her legs, another half-ton of fury. Winter felt a grinding inside him; this was *vero* hand-to-hand, a true test, and with the deadliest opponent of all, a sow-bitch.

The beast came at him, trampling and spurning the twitching body of the bull with her chisel hooves. Her mouth was gaping, showing huge, jagged teeth which could crack rock. Winter teetered back and forth in half-steps, trying to time the momentum of her charge. He held his arms high, flashed them down when the jaws were a foot away, seized her heavy ears and yanked himself up and over the snout in a half-gainer like a Cretan bull-dancer, and was mounted on the sow's back, clutching the thick hair.

She bucked, pitched, and yawed high in the light gravity. He held fast with legs and one hand while with the other he drew the Slice Knife. He cut the lady's throat.

He brought both hearts back to the Maori dome spitted on the blade of Te Uinta's spear.

o   o   o

It was a joyous celebration. Winter was the first ever to bring off a double kill, and that was welcomed as a glorious omen. He was indeed Double-King R-og, and the proof was the two hearts roasting over a fire.

There were drums pounding, not in classic Terran 2/4, 3/4, and 4/4 rhythms, but in traditional Maori style which has no regular beat because they're telling a story, with punctuation, pauses, comments and elaborations.

There were girls and women dancing, again not

in structured Terran steps. They too were acting out ancient Maori sagas with symbolic gestures telling of wars won, enemies conquered, heroes mating and producing mighty child-men who would someday lead the Maori to even greater victories.

There was feasting; young crocodile, probably stolen from the Afro Domes, anaconda, ten-pound frogs, imported shark, mule, and barbecued mammoth. No point in leaving those two carcasses for their friends and relations to devour. And there was opium and hemp bought from the Turkish Domes.

With exquisite timing, before the festival could start falling apart, the shaman conducted Winter to the platform on which he'd been crowned, standing on his father's shield. Now the two mammoth hearts were roasting on it. This was the climax.

The shaman bowed, stepped down, and joined the tribal chiefs circling the earthen dais. Winter picked up the spit, burning his hands but refusing to flinch before his people. He took a giant bite out of the first heart, chewed the scorching meat, again without flinching, and swallowed. Pandemonium! He repeated the ritual with the second heart but this time the joy was cut off in mid-shout. He looked around at his people in amazement and then at the shaman and chieftains who were backing away from the dais in terror.

"What?" he called.

The shaman could only point at Rogue's feet.

He looked down. The platform was crawling

with small living things emerging from the earth. They had no discernible shape. They were grey, hairy mounds that seemed to blunder aimlessly in search of something.

"Mammoth souls!" a horrified voice cried from the crowd. "They're the mammoth souls. Souls of the royal kills."

Winter was badly shaken by this unknown but couldn't reveal it. Certainly a king couldn't back away in fright. In the heavy silence, he repeated the ceremonial eating of the hearts, replaced the spit, turned and strode slowly and proudly off the dais, never deigning to look down at the mysteries creeping underfoot. Yael says it was a superb performance, and back in the royal palace he congratulated Rogue.

"Thanks, Jay. My God, I was scared."

"So was I."

"D'you believe in life after death? Ghosts? Revenants? That sort of occult?"

"Certainly not for animals."

"Me neither. Then what were those things crawling around my feet? Not mammoth souls."

"We'll find out," Yael said. "I've got one."

"What?"

"I grabbed a 'soul' when we started back to the palace."

"Where is it?"

"Right here."

Yael opened his ceremonial cloak, shook a fold, and down dropped a small, grey, hairy mound which began an uncertain crawling. "Looks like mammoth hide," Yael murmured. He touched the top of the creeping mound, explored gently, twitched it once and then picked it up, revealing what was underneath.

"Why, it's a baby horseshoe crab covered with mammoth hide," he exclaimed.

"Don't touch it," Winter said sharply. "That's no baby crab. It's a mature Kring centipede with a carapace, and it's deadly poisonous."

Yael jerked back out of danger. Winter stood up and crushed the creature with one powerful stamp of his shod foot. Then he began to pace.

"So that's the picture," he said at last.

"What picture, son?"

"Look at it, Jay. Kringpedes are underground types. What's under the kampong and dais?"

"The Dome power plant."

"So they came up from there."

"It seems likely."

"Where they could be caught, put into mysterious costume, and teased into burrowing up to me on the dais."

"That's rather extreme, son."

"Jay, an overt hit on me was tried before I was crowned. They still want me wiped but now that I'm official royalty it can't be overt anymore. There'd be hell to pay."

"True."

"Then how about a poisoning by dead souls? King R-og must have offended the gods and been punished. The superstitious Maori would buy that and make no objections to his succession."

"That terrorist group again?"

"Still, Jay, still." He shook his head doggedly.

"I've got to settle this or there'll never be peace."

"Have you any idea who they are, Rogue?"

"Not the faintest."

"Then how can you settle it?"

"I'm going down into the power plant after them. That's strictly off-limits, so it's probably their cell. Certainly they sent the doom of the gods up from there. See you, Jay," and he was gone.

The plant was an enormous dark cellar crowded with what seemed to be upright steel boilers with friendly arms around each others' shoulders. In fact they were the linked energy units, all in locked armor casing to protect them from damage and tampering. Lantern light glowed near the center of the plant, but Winter's view was blocked by the silhouetted boiler units. He advanced silently, threading and twisting through the maze, one hand on the hilt of the ritual Slice Knife which he still wore. The sound of low voices came; then full view.

Three women and two men around a lantern in close conference. His heart wrenched and he shook his head again. "But I should have guessed," he thought. The women were his stepsisters. Winter stepped forward into the lantern light, making no attempt to walk silently. The five turned and saw who it was. There was a long moment of confrontation. All of them understood.

Winter motioned to the men. "Go," he said. "This is a family affair."

The men hesitated until his sisters nodded. Winter and the women were left alone.

After another silence he said, "I should have

known when you didn't show at the coronation, but I was occupied with so many new things."

No answer.

"Kuiti, Tapanu, Patea, you're all looking well."

They were; tall, handsome women in their late forties, starting to grey, not yet gone to fat.

"But why? Why?"

"We are the only true bloodline."

"And I'm only an adopted orphan. Yes, Kuiti, but you've always known that."

"And hated it," Tapanu said.

"I don't blame you. I know I'm an outsider, an intruder; but it was never my wish, it was your father's."

"He had no right."

"He had every right, Patea. No woman can ever sit on the throne."

"We have husbands."

"Ah, so that's it. And sons?"

Their silence was the answer.

"I see. I'm sorry. The direct Uinta line is ended. Too bad, but it's happened to many royal lines in the past. So you'll elevate one of your husbands and be the power behind the throne. What if he won't listen? What then?"

"He'll listen. We are three, the true children of Te Uinta."

"Of course, but whose husband will it be? Yours, Kuiti? You're the oldest."

"You murdered him," she snapped.

"Murdered? Nonsense!"

"On Venucci."

"On Ven—? You mean . . . what was his name?

Kea Ora? I thought he was just a soldier."

"He was the next king."

Winter was stunned. "My God! My God! What a disaster! My sister's husband . . . "

"Never your sister."

"And now never a king. What about those men who were here with you? Husbands, too?"

"No."

"Soldiers?"

"Yes."

"They looked it. How many have you in your group?"

"You'll find out when we're ready."

"No, Kuiti," he answered slowly. "No, you'll never be ready, now that I know and can have you called to account no matter what happens to me. Dear sisters, loving sisters, Kuiti, Tapanu, Patea, you're finished."

"Never!"

"Finished," he repeated. He drew the Slice Knife. They never flinched. "If anything happens to me or mine, you'll be held accountable. My sacred blood oath on it." He slashed his forearm and before they could avoid it, smeared his blood on their faces.

"My sworn blood on your heads," he said. "This is the end of your vendetta. We'll never meet again."

He turned and left them, but as he disappeared in the dark he called back, "You never once spoke my name."

Chapter Five

LOVELORN

'Tis said that absence conquers love,
   But oh! Believe it not;
I've tried, alas! its power to prove,
   But thou art not forgot.
          —Frederick William Thomas

This is Odessa Partridge again, on Terra, in the Northeast Corridor, reminding you that I'm putting all this together in sequence from what the principals confided in me much later. It makes me feel like a Yiddisha Mama, and I love it.

While R-grunt-OG was working out his destiny on Ganymede, *une crise se prépare* (a "things coming to a head") clobbered Demi Jeroux in the New York jungle. I'd explained the urgency of Rogue's abrupt departure, and she'd accepted it without complaint like the good child that she was. Now, while she was waiting for his return, she was trying to go through the motions of her life as it had been before the trapper became the trappee.

But she woke up this morning, upchucking in all directions for the second time, and again passed it off as a lovelorn stomach. She examined her fresh-woke basic Titanian reality in the mirror and was again amazed to see Winter's ideal; slender, virginal, with a big befront and a high inhind. Limpid skin and auburn hair, she might have been Botticelli's model for "The Birth of Venus" if

Sandro hadn't desexed his vision.

"So this is what Rogue's done to me," she murmured. "They never talk about the Frog Princess." She turned to the psycat. "I've made a profound discovery; a woman needs a man to make her real."

Titanian constraints imposed a dress style on her which career women around the Solar will understand. She had to wear clothes which would not clash with any guise she might be obliged to transform into during her work; competent, helpless, shrewd, maneuvering, ego-trip, team-player, etc. She selected a dark unobtrusive suit, quiet buttoned blouse, sensible shoes, no ornaments, but in her tote she carried jewelry and an evening purse and evening sandals just in case. She switched on the kaleidoscope projector for the entertainment of the psycat spot-chaser and left for the *Media* office.

Demi was working the "Soft Shift" this month, noon to six, but she was dedicated and often put in extra morning hours. She needed them this day because she was required to cope with submissions in Nü-Spēk, Medieval French, Mozambique, Arcane English, and Chromatics, and forward them to *Media*'s owner and editor-in-chief, Augustus (Ching) Sterne, with crisp descriptions and explicit recommendations. She'd been particularly tickled by the lunacy of "Rabelais Diabolo," proving that François was Satan in disguise (she knew that the great medieval *farceur* had been a Titanian) but Ching was not amused.

By five-thirty she decided that an evening on the

town would help her forget Rogue for a few hours, so she dialed *GIRLGUARD*, waited for the computer to check her credit, and ordered an escort who would be Winter's exact opposite. That, she imagined, would squelch office gossip. To the crucial specification, Sex? she hammered an emphatic NO which, of course, was noted by the office and only confirmed the tittle-tattle.

He strutted into *Media*, small, powerful, aggressive—you could almost see the chip on his shoulder—with an attitude that announced he was God's gift to the Solar and you'd better believe it. "Miz Jeroux?" he challenged. "Miz Demi Jeroux?"

"Here," Demi answered while her heart sank.

"I'm Samson from GIRLGUARD." He made it sound like a commercial while his eyes took in the other women on the floor. "Herc Samson."

"Herc for Hercules?" a small voice called from a corner.

"You got it, babe," Samson threw over his shoulder. He took Demi's elbow. "Leave us hit the highs, honey." He grinned. "Your credit's gonna take one beautiful beating but don't worry, Herc'll make everything worth it." He cased her. "Too bad about that negatory, babe. You look like you could use Herc. He's the greatest. Herc's the works."

Demi wanted something different from the cultivated entertainment to which she was accustomed, so Samson gave her a wild tour of the Northeast underworld. He was intimate with cracksmen and fences, magsmen, goniffs, and shofulmen, the swell mob, the fancy sportsmen and sporting houses, the citadels of the under-world. "I'm the greatest, honey," he assured her. "You're guaranteed girlguarded, so don't worry. Herc's the works."

She quailed at the entertainments of the sporting fancy, first at The Hound Hut.

Raising a really first-class fighting dog is a serious business. Mastiffs, bulldogs, terriers, hounds, huskies, setters, airedales, and savage crossbreeds are imported from the entire Solar, most of them stolen. Since they're fought by weight, about forty to fifty pounds is the maximum so that ten in the pit will not exceed five hundred pounds.

Careful feeding and training is vital. Practice encounters introduce the dog to its profession. "Taste Goons," poor, indentured laborers, are fed up to give them some strength and spirit (some-times with the promise of manumission) and used. Before being put into the practice pit the Taste Goon has the most vulnerable parts of his body shaved so that the dog can learn to attack these places.

Demi stared around with wide eyes as Samson led her into the pit parlor. Center was the round, deep circus with a sand floor, surrounded by crowded bleachers. Sporting prints hung on the walls. There were glassed vitrines containing stuffed dogs, famous in their day. They flanked a large portrait of what seemed to be a nude blackamoor jockey, "Wonder Timmy."

"Weighed a hundred pounds," Samson told Demi. "Always wore a woman's bracelet around his neck. Timmy once fought three mains in a row. He was the greatest killer of all time, but they got him in the end."

At one side of the pit, half a dozen nude and shaven men were warming up with ferocious calisthenics while shouting and screaming gamblers were laying odds on their favorites. The first main was called and "Bendigo Benny" announced. Benny vaulted heavily into the pit and paraded in a circle while his backers cheered and applauded. He took center and nodded to the M.C. A chute opened, ten snarling, slavering fighting dogs swarmed into the circus and tore at Bendigo Benny as he began kicking and smashing them to death.

"Can we go, please?" Demi whispered.

"You sound like a pet freak, honey," Samson laughed. "That's okay. Everything's perk with Herc. Tell you what, we'll try a Shoot'em'up. No dogs."

The BBOH (Bitches & Bastards of Outlaw History) stages its entertainments in a replica of a Western saloon. The members re-create the legendary 20th-century Western stars; Gary Cooper, Jimmy Stewart, "Duke" Wayne, Marlene Dietrich, Mae West, etc. Great pains are taken with the costumes, and the men practice quick-draw with six-guns while the women rehearse tough seduction and the barroom cancan. The gambling types wear shiny top hats, frock coats, and practice various forms of card manipulation and cheating in the style of John Carradine, Henry Hull, Brian Donlevy, *et al.*

This night they were staging a barroom brawl, featuring broken furniture, shattered glass, bloody fistfights, thrown bottles, and finally a gun-walk and quickdraw encounter which ended with the shooting of Henry Fonda wearing a star and Jane Russell wearing nothing.

"They make it seem so real!" Demi exclaimed, applauding enthusiastically.

"It *is* real, baby."

"What? Those people . . . really hurt and . . . and killed?"

"Uh-huh, they're really clobbered. All the fighting's for real. They love to maul each other. That's why the BBOH is a sellout."

"And . . . and the killing?"

"No, they don't go that far. It's faked with high-power props that look realer than the real thing and cost a mint. That's why tickets are priced out of sight. You're going to scream when you see what we've been charged. Herc's no jerk. He always delivers."

"Can we go, please?"

"But baby, a lynching comes next."

"Please?"

"Okay. How about a classy courtroom trial? No dogs, no assault and battery. Just good clean fun."

It was a sporting house decorated in the plush Victorian style; red velvet, cut glass, fumed oak, flickering gaslight. The brothel bullies wore tailcoats and starched white bibs studded with diamonds. There was even a Victorian governess chaperoning the child prostitutes.

They were holding one of their featured mock trials for an enthusiastic paying audience. A court-

room had been set up in the LSD lounge. There
was a Victorian judge in black robes and white
wig on the bench, wielding a circumcised dildo
gavel. Up in the musicians gallery the band was
playing gems from "Trial by Jury." Twelve
sequinned whores sat in the jury box, powdered
and rouged, and enticingly décolleté. The accused
before the judge was another grotesquely painted
whore and was singing, screaming and rhyming on
a mad trip.

"Prisoner," the judge shouted over the uproar,
"you have been charged. What have you to say in
your offense?"

"How did *you* get to be my judge?" she
demanded and sang, "Oh judge not, pussy, lest ye
be judged, coozy, lest ye be bugged, riff, fugged,
riff, hugged, riff, mugged—"

The dildo pounded. "Don't you know,
prisoner?"

"Oh I know, I know, with a bribe. On the path."

"What path?"

"The Bridal Path. How many legs does a horse
have?"

"Four."

"If you take three legs from the Four Whores-
men of the Apocalypse how many are left?"

"Nine."

"Subtract prix your goner and what's left?"

"Three."

"I have three legs which makes me a horse."

"Whose horse, prisoner?"

"Everybody's. Take two from me and what's
left?"

"One."

"The one and only, the be all and end all, riff, the sweet end, raff, the beat end, ruff, sentence me, sentence me to fart labor."

"Prisoner at the bar, I sentence you to rape."

"Oh goody, goody bum drops. A rape is a wake is a cake is a jape is a gape which is mine for one and all, come one, come all, come, come, come until you're squeezed dry."

She stripped, revealing that she was a fag in drag and the jury, leaping upon him while the audience cheered and jeered, revealed the same thing.

"And that's why the ambassador blew his brains out," Samson told the horrified Demi.

"Wh-what?"

"Tröyj Caliph, the Turkish ambassador. The embassy claimed it was a heart attack, but he really suzysided. Got trapped in the badger game by the swell mob. You know, babe. Pick up a hustler. Go to her place for jollies. Get caught flagrant plus tapes which you buy off. But the mob wasn't selling, they set him up for blackmail. Can you guess how?"

"I . . . I d-don't want to."

"They pulled a fancy switch on the ambassador. The hustler wasn't a real doll, it was that one down there, the prisoner getting banged. Fagsville. Panic city for Tröyj . . ."

"Please," Demi begged. "I want to go home now."

She was girlguarded back to her apartment, signed Samson's careful bills, safed the door and collapsed.

o   o   o

(Postscript to Demi's adventures: We'd been plagued by the Turkish Domes on Ganymede for years, demanding an explanation of that bewildering suicide. When Demi finally told me about her night on the town, it solved the mystery. Since Rogue was responsible, in a way, for her sordid evening out, he'd more or less played "Pointer" for us again.)

o   o   o

Demi awoke next morning, sick again with additional complications. There was no doubt that she had to see a doctor. She reported in sick to the *Media* office, called her real mother in Virginia, and took off for a consultation.

Now, you're a Titanian polymorph. You're a voluntary expatriate because you prefer life on Terra, as many Titanians have down through the ages, and you enjoy your role as a respected physician. What is the permanent persona you adopt? What do you think a lady doctor should look like? Demi's mother, Dr. Althea Lenox, had taken the great queen, Elizabeth of England, as her model.

The consultation was in Titanian, of course. Since it's impossible to depict a chemical conversation on paper, I'll leave it blank and you can fill in with three of your senses; taste, touch, and smell. It won't be easy; Titanian grammar is tricky. For example, the feel of wool cannot be used as the verb for the smell of wood smoke unless the object of the sentence has a pleasant flavor.

There was only one Terran word spoken during those three days:

"Rabbit."

Demi returned to New York, terrified.

o   o   o

In Demi's apartment, Winter finished the excited account of his adventures on Ganymede and disengaged the psycat's embrace around his neck. She'd been captivated, either by him, the vibes of his voice, or the promise of eye spots in the future. Rogue cosseted her on his lap and examined Demi perplexedly, somewhat surprised by her appearance or, more specifically, her lack of appearance.

After a three-week separation he'd expected her to greet him transformed into the role of the vivacious hostess, perhaps even her namesake, Madame Jeanne Françoise Julie Adélaide Récamier (1777-1840), entertaining literary and political society in her fashionable salon. Instead, Demi looked washed-out. She asked a few indifferent questions.

"And Dr. Yael?"

"I left him behind as my regent."

"Will you have to go back?"

"I'm not sure. Certainly next year, for another kill."

"Did you—have to eat the heart?"

"Both. My people nearly went out of their minds. I'm a double-king and, by God, I'm proud of it. I certainly earned it."

(He was and had indeed and, most significant of all, had abandoned the masking spectacles.)

"And that girl?" Demi asked. "The one you— Did you see her again?"

"Ah-ha!" he exclaimed. "So that's it."

"That's what?"

"Why you're so cold tonight. No, I never saw her again. Odessa Partridge was right; the hit-crowd got lost after the coronation." He didn't think it wise to worry her with an account of the confrontation with his stepsisters. "And please believe me, love, absolutely nothing happened between me and their zapette; no bang, just a bite on her ass to teach her a lesson. So no jealousy, please. Warm up and look me one of your looks that I've been missing for weeks."

"I'm not cold, Rogue, just tired and depressed, and you're on a high roll, so please to go home, dear, and leave me alone."

"You never called me 'dear' before, it was always 'darling.' Why now?"

"Please stop nagging me."

"What's wrong? You're so nervous."

"No I'm not."

"And you've got that same expression you had when you propositioned me in the conference room, scared but determined."

"No I don't."

"Come on, tell Daddy what it's all about. Give me three guesses. You've been fired."

"No."

"You're in love with another guy and don't know how to hand me my *congé.*"

"Don't joke."

"You owe money. You're being dunned."

"Nothing like that."

"I give up, You'll have to tell Daddy."

"You won't let it alone?"

"No. Stand and deliver."

She took a deep breath and firmed her lips. "All right, Daddy. You're a Daddy."

"What!"

"I'm pregnant." She began to cry.

He was incredulous. "But you said it's never happened between Terrans and Titanians."

"N-never, b-but I suppose there always has to be a first."

"You said our eggs and sperms don't love each other."

"Maybe I l-love you so much that it—it sort of magicked us. I don't know." She was sobbing. "Maybe jus 'nother c-cosmic joke and n-not funny."

"How'd you find out?"

"I— I m-missed my period last week and—"

"You have them?" he broke in.

"All females do . . . and usually I'm like clockwork. So I went to m-my mother—my real doctor mother—and she made some tests and . . . and you know now, and I'm scared to death. I don't know what to do."

Winter let out a sustained yell. The psycat scatted off his lap.

"Rogue! The neighbors!"

"One night. Knocked up in one glorious night. By God, we'll beat the insects yet! Come here, Starmom. Come on!" He enfolded her. "If it's a boy he'll be named after both my fathers, Te Jay. If it's a girl she'll be named after all of you, Demure Delicious Double-jointed Gay Deceiver Demi. We'll call her Decalcomania for short. There's only one problem," he added, "owing to a surfeit of tradition."

"What?"

"The sunbursts. He'll be King Te Jay Uinta, eventually. Is it fair to put a boy through the royal cheek-bit?" His hand reached in the automatic tic for the spectacles he wasn't wearing.

"That isn't the problem."

"Think not?"

"I know not. The problem is, will he *be* a boy? Will she *be* a girl? What will the hybrid be?"

"What the hell do I care? He, she, or it will be ours, and that's enough for me. You know, I *thought* you'd put on weight."

"After a week? Don't be silly."

"You will, you will, and then—Hoop-la!"

"I thought you'd be scared, too."

"Are you mad? I've spent my life synergizing other people's patterns. Now we've got our own personal, home-grown, brand-new pattern to play with, Ms. Winter."

She was laughing and crying. "Rogue Winter,

this is the damnedest marriage proposal I've ever had, and I've had plenty. At the office the betting was that you'd wind up marrying a high-fashion model."

"Yeh, I know that zokamamie syndrome. The sophisticated beauty who turns everybody's head in the ski lodge. All girls are haunted by her. Usually she's named Mystique d'Charisma."

"Do be serious, Rogue."

"What's to be serious? Look at it. Odessa Partridge has cooled it with the Bologna fuzz. The Maori wipe is out, now that I been kinged. And the kid—whatever kind of weirdo we produce—will be a prince or a princess. This is a jaunty prologue to a jolly adventure."

"It's the weird that's frightening me. It's all new, the first time, so even my mother can't advise me, and I do need advice . . . desperately. Please help me find it, Rogue."

He nodded and thought hard for a long time, long enough for the smitten psycat to nestle back into his lap. "Tomas Young," he said with decision. "He's your man."

"A doctor?"

"Better. Tomas is director of the Exobiology department at the university. He's *the* mavin on the nature of all possible life-forms and their genesis. I did a piece once on the crazy life-constructs he and his crazy computer created. If you boned up on me to hook me, like you said, you probably read it."

"Will you ask him to advise me?"

"He'll be delighted, darling. Tom loves a

challenge, and this one's a beauty. I'll see him first thing in the morning and set it up. Oh, one warning: Tom's a trustable gent, in case you have to strip for an examination, but watch out for that computer. It's a goddam letch."

"Ssss."

"So now let's go to bed, love. Please?"

"I thought you'd go home to unpack."

"Why d'you think I came straight here from the port?"

"Unga-unga-unga."

"What the hell's that?"

"Ssss in Maori," and she began to transform into her idea of the hamstringing zapette.

Chapter Six

More Deceivers

Love no man; trust no man: speak ill of no man to his face, nor well of any man behind his back. Spread yourself upon his bosom publicly, whose heart you would eat in private.

—Ben Jonson

I fell in love with "Soho" Young, which was the name Tomas used when I first met him, the time my roommate wanted to lose her virginity. We were Seven Sister freshmen, from "good" families, and I was a virgin, too, but never admitted it. Alas, well-brought-up boys never try to go all the way with nice girls, and that's all we ever got to meet.

We were in the Jungle-Mother exploring the single bars and drinking too much and too damn clumsy and shy to pick up a man or even recognize that we were the pickups occasionally. Couple of nice, naïve kids full of rude health and clean living.

Anyway, Marj was determined to get rid of "it" at a posh stud place advertised in a handout offered to us in the street, but we'd run out of large money. However, we hadn't run out of bravado so we decided to hock something. I knew about as much about hockshops as I did about men but off we went, the two vivandieres, and luck, fate, or The Great Pawnbroker in the Sky led us to Soho Young's Loan Shop just as he was closing up.

He looked like Ivan the Terrible and later I wondered whether Young was a shortening of some impossible Mongol name. He wasn't too enthusiastic about this late rush, but we explained that we had to get back to school that night and had run out of money for fare and could he please help us raise fifty. Soho cocked an eye and said, "Fifty? You Chicago? Northwestern?"

I cleverly covered up. "No, Mr. Young. Maine. University of."

"Must be going by boat," Soho said. "What've you got?"

We offered our "sensible" jewelry, the little that our families would let us wear, and Soho disdained everything but touched my wristwatch with a finger. "That's an antique Patek. Man's. Your father's?"

"Yes, Mr. Young."

"He shouldn't let you wear it. Too good for a freshman."

Marj blurted, "How'd you know we—"

Soho's knowing eye cut her off. "I can lend you fifty on this," he told me. He slid a ticket across the counter and showed me how to fill it in and instructed me how to reclaim the watch. He handed me two twenties and a ten. "All gig?"

I nodded. He hesitated, inspected us glancingly, then permitted a crease to turn up a corner of his mouth. He opened a tiny cabinet behind the cash register. It was full of medicines and he took out a small white box and gave it to me. "Bonus," he said. "Cordial customer relations."

"Thank you, Mr. Young." I was bewildered.

"What is it?"

"Seasick pills," he said and hustled us out of the Loan Shop. On the street I opened the box. It contained four "*senza*'s," Venucci oral contraceptive pills. How in God's name did that amazing man know? I gave the pills to Marj while I gave my heart to Soho Young.

I redeemed the watch the next time I was in the Jungle and only much later discovered that Soho had done something very generous; he'd had it cleaned and renovated for me. When I tried to thank him he brushed me off. "Didn't do it for you, did it for the watch. You're just a kid; you don't realize how precious an old watch is. They got to be treasured like rare paintings, so don't be wearing it when you're back-and-forth-handing on the goddam tennis team." That was typical of him; he'd quietly checked me out and knew all about me.

There isn't much difference between pawnbrokers and psychiatrists. Soho knew all about everything, which made him the kind of father that a girl dreams of; experienced, sophisticated, never at a loss, never judging, never without a wry sense of humor. I infested his place every chance I got and spent hours watching and listening and receiving an education whenever Soho was there, which wasn't often; he seemed to leave most of the business to his clerks.

I remember that crease quirking in the corner of his mouth when he said that he'd have preferred to send me to Yale. My school was, in his opinion, a fag-dyke school, and Matthew Vassar's beer had been undrinkable. To cure me of piss-elegant campus culture, Soho administered strong doses of hockshop reality.

For instance, there was a bona fide Indian princess with the red dot on her forehead, the sari, and practically everything else except "Indian Love Lyrics" by Amy Woodforde-Finden. She pulled into the Loan Shop one afternoon wearing a brand-new mink coat. Without a word she took it off and put it on the counter. Soho glanced at it and handed her fifteen hundred. She left without counting the cash.

"She comes in every month with a new coat," he explained as he wrapped it up. "Her mother's a maharanee or something from Ganymede. Loaded. They got charge accounts at all the expensive stores, but the old lady won't give her daughter an allowance. So the princess, she just charges a new coat and hocks it for spending money. I figure her mother pays bills without bothering to read them. That loaded." Soho gave me a stern look. "I think the princess, she uses the money to buy rough studs off the street, and I know she's got V.D. Let that be a lesson to you."

"Yes, Mr. Young," I said.

One bright morning a young man in black tie and bombed out of his brain came in carrying a beautiful antique lantern clock. Soho allowed him two hundred on it and he staggered out with the money. I started to ask something, but Soho motioned me to wait. A few moments later an excessively English butler entered, paid two hundred plus interest on the loan and departed with the clock. The entire transaction had been as silent and automatic as that with the Ganymede princess.

"Dutch kid from Callisto," Soho explained. "Rich. Always needs money for skag, so he steals something from the house. I got an arrangement with his mother. She guarantees any loan I make him."

"But if she knows what he's doing, why doesn't she give him the money herself?"

"She can't get him off horse, so she figures the least she can do is make him sweat for his smack." Soho gave me another steely look. "He picked up the habit in *your* fag-dyke college. Let that be a lesson to you and watch yourself. Only habit you should have is work."

"Thank you, Mr. Young."

Soho's slogan was: If it isn't alive and you can get it through the door, you can hock it. His clerks, Roland and Eli showed me the damnedest things that were brought in; animal heads, outboard motors, an entire gypsy cimbalom, a python skin forty feet long. One old character pawned fourteen sets of false teeth, not his own. Soho never did find out how he got them.

"Craziest thing that ever came in was a mummy," he told me.

"A mummy? Like from a pyramid?"

"Gig. My first thought was, this guy zigged it from some museum, so I checked."

"How, Mr. Young?"

"Pay attention and learn. Mummies are so special they're all pedigreed. The experts know every one."

"Oh. Like vintage cars, Mr. Young?"

"Now you dig it. This one was legit. The guy was an Egyptologist trying to raise money for another expedition up the Nile or wherever. So I let him have fifteen thousand."

"Did he redeem it?"

"No. Wrote and told me to sell it."

"Did you get your money back?"

"Now you go too far," Soho said sternly.

"Sorry, Mr. Young."

But behind him Eli silently raised a thumb and forefinger for a "two" and then ringed them into a "zero" and jerked his hand four times.

One glorious afternoon Soho permitted me to stand in the pledge cage as an acting clerk. "Teach you something you can't learn in that fag-dyke school," he said, "How to size people up. Half the Solar is goniffs conniving to rip the other half." Of course his assistants kept a watchful eye on me, but my first customer was an astonishing lesson in human "idio-nys-canaries," as Soho always put it, which no one could possibly have predicted.

An engineer off one of the Solar ships—his radiation badge read, "CUNARD BRIGADIER"—rolled in, obviously enjoying a Happy Hour, and asked, "Hoi, you jocks hock any whatsoever?"

"If it isn't alive and you can get it through the door," I parroted, "you can pawn it."

"R," he said and planked a Lloyd's thousand banknote down on the cage counter before me. "Wanna hock this."

I stared. "You want to pawn cash?"

He grinned. "Gotta red-hot momma in tow. Don't want her find out got this much on me. Sure to take me. Leave it where's safe. R?"

I looked at Eli and Roland. They shrugged and nodded, so I started filling out a ticket. "How much do you want on this, sailor?"

"Nothin'. Jussa ticket."

"It'll cost you the standard five percent all the same."

"A-Oke." He fished a five out of his pocket and handed it over. "Sort of protection money, har? Pay five, save a milli." He received his ticket and rolled out singing, *"He knew the world was round-O, he knew it could be found-O..."*

An hour later the red-hot momma came in with the ticket and collected the thousand.

Soho's clerks told me that small-time crooks devote a lot of time and thought to ripping pawnbrokers. They hock painted diamonds, rings with doublet stones (glass with a sliver of diamond cemented on top to pass the scratch test), dummy cameras from window displays, and watches and accordions without internal works. Roland said, "They pick the rush hours when everyone's crowding the buffet and we haven't the time to look inside the sandwiches." Roland had a sort of Madison Avenue advertisingese nostalgia, which he got mixed up occasionally. Once I heard him say, "Let's run it up the flagpole and see if it gets off at Grand Central."

When respectables visited the hockshop for the first time, they were usually ashamed, imagining that they were at the bottom of the financial line and groveling in the gutter. This always annoyed Soho, who told me, "Man's got a mortgage on his home and he isn't ashamed. So why should he be ashamed of a mortgage on his watch? Answer me that, girlie."

"I can't, Mr. Young."

"Did you and your friend who wanted to get laid feel that way when you come in the first time? Did she?"

"She wasn't ashamed, Mr. Young."

"I don't mean that. Did she get to use the Seasick pills?"

"Oh. Yes. Just in case. That was very nice of y—"

"Like it?"

"I think she was scared more than anything else, Mr. Young."

"Uh-huh. Figures. Were you ashamed, hocking your watch?"

"No, Mr. Young. It was an adventure."

"Uh-huh. Got to get *you* fixed up soon. Nice girl like you. You're overdue."

"Oh, Mr. Young . . . "

"Romantic, that's your problem. At Yale your ass would have been banged off seventeen ways to Tuesday by now. Run up a score before you fall in love. Dig? Fag-dyke college!"

But I'd done so brilliantly my first year at fag-dyke Vassar—and I really do believe that it was Soho's dynamic influence that drove me—that the *TerraGardai* Section contacted me at the beginning of the sophomore term and I began my long association with Intelligence. And Soho Young abruptly disappeared. Pouf! Just like that. *Spurlos versenkt.* Without realizing it, much less intending it, I'd made his ancillary decoy cover too dangerous to continue. Intelligence (bureaucrats prefer to call us the *TerraGardai* Section) didn't brief me on that until long after the event.

And that late, great Soho Young was the same Tomas Young, exobiologist, whom Winter was to consult on Demi Jeroux's behalf. I can hear Winter now: "Who? Whom? I busted pronouns owing to a surfeit of————." Fill in the missing word and you may win one of five giant cash prizes.

o   o   o

"To my knowledge I've never seen a Titanian, Rogue. Of course I must have—they've filtered all through the Solar—but I couldn't know. How'd you spot your loved one?"

"I didn't, Tom."

"She tell you?"

"She showed me."

"Fascinating. I'd love to have a look inside her."

"No way."

"Just a little peek? It wouldn't hurt."

"Forget it."

"Oh well, I'll settle for the Roentgen caper."

"Will that do anything to her?"

"How should I know?"

"Then it's out."

"Selfish! How'd your sprite find out she was pregnant for sure?"

"Tests."

"Then she's seen a doctor. *He'll* make a splash in

the medical journals. First time a physician's ever had the chance to examine a Titanian. Either they're outrageously healthy or they go home for treatment."

"It was a lady doctor."

"Then *she'll* make the headlines."

"Demi's mother. Titanian."

"What? I wonder how the Terran Medical Association will take that when they find out?"

"We're not going to snitch. Now look, Tom, d'you want to advise my Demi or not? It's *your* big chance to make a splash."

"No internal examination?"

"Tom! I love the girl. I won't have her running the chance of getting hurt."

"You drive a hard bargain."

"Don't try to bamboozle me. I'm a king."

"So I hear. *Le Roi Malgré lui.* Big two-hearted ruler. When do they chop your head off?"

"What's that damn noise?"

"The think-tank. It gets lonely."

"You spoil it."

"I catch more lemmas with sugar than vinegar." Young dropped the light tone and spoke sincerely. "Gig, Rogue. I'm honored and grateful that you came to me. I want very much to meet your Titanian girl, and I swear that I'll do nothing that could possibly hurt her."

"Then how are you going to help her?"

"Ask personal questions to find out whether her anabolic and catabolic functions parallel Terran metabolism. If they do, great and not to worry. If they don't, then ask more questions and feed her data to Goody Gumdrops in there. We'll come up with a prognosis and a regimen for your Demi. She said they pop them out like shelling peas?"

Rogue nodded.

"Then cool it. The computer and Demi and I will cope, while you're pacing the hospital waiting room. There's really only one fascinating puzzle; how long will her pregnancy last? We need a solid nine months to develop the normal Terran kid, but how long a term will your double-endowed half-breed miracle require? Nine? Ten? Twelve?"

"Oi."

"I think I'll headline the first scoop: My Terranian And How It Grew."

"This is no joke for me, Tom."

"And this is the last thing I ever expected from you. The expectant father. Feeling any labor pains yet?"

"I'd better get Demi over here right away."

"Cool the rush, Rogue. You may have a year and a half before she pops. Come inside and type '+HELLO+' on the terminal to the Lemma Meshugenah. That'll give it fits and get it off my back for a while."

"Why don't you?"

"Mumbo Jumbo knows my touch on the keyboard."

"The trouble with you two is that you're having an illikit love-hate affair."

Winter tore himself away from Young's blandishments, too cheered by the reassurances to sense the ugly pattern that was shaping. Love will do that to the best; they lose their grasp on reality.

As a rule, when a *Garda* becomes spellbound I give him or her a forced sabbatical. But I'm not proud of my own performance in the action. With twenty-twenty hindsight I see now that I should have twigged the setup. How could Tomas Young know about the coronation double-kill? Winter had spent the night with Demi Jeroux and spoken to no one else when he returned from Ganymede.

He was close to caracolling on his way to bring the good news from Young to Jeroux. It occurred to him that his sprite of the unexpected might have gone to the *Media* office despite her promise to stay home, but no matter; they had exchanged keys after that first night, and if she wasn't in he could call from her place, pretending it was business. The fine Virginia girl didn't want any public intimacy until they had a social status.

"A ring!" Winter exclaimed. "An engagement ring. That's the answer."

He began to window-shop along the same main drag where he had encountered Twelve Drummers Drumming three weeks before. In the busy vitrine of a jewelry boutique he saw a small gold seal ring. He looked at it for a long moment, muttered, "Could be," and pressed the button alongside the door. After a brief inspection by the owner, the door lock was released and Winter was admitted.

"Good morning. I'd like to have a look at that seal ring in your window. Second row from the bottom, third from the left."

The ring was placed on a velvet cushion on the counter. It was pinkish gold, fairly heavy, and engraved with a four-petal blossom in deep intaglio.

"Would that be a dogwood design?" Winter asked.

"Yes, sir. Pink flowering dogwood."

"I thought so."

"That's why pink gold was used. It's a rare antique. Red and pink golds haven't been seen on the market in centuries."

"The Belgians are smelting it on Callisto," Winter said, "but I suppose they're keeping it all for themselves. I'll take the ring." He had no worries about it fitting Demi's finger; that would be child's play for a Titanian.

After the nuisance of finger- and eyeprint identification and a bank check, Winter departed with the wrapped ring. "Dogwood is the state flower of Virginia," he told the proprietor. "I would have gotten an 'A' in botany if I hadn't busted it, owing to a surfeit of poison ivy."

Chapter Seven

THE LAMMISTER

lam (lam) v. lammed, lamming, n. *Slang.*
—v.t. 1. to run away quickly.—n. 2. on the
lam, fleeing or hiding, esp. from the police.
—The Random House Dictionary

Winter bounced up the stairs and rang Demi's doorbell. After a moment the door was opened by what appeared to be a good-looking street stud.

"Can I help you?" the man asked.

"Oh, sorry," Winter said. "I must have stopped at the wrong floor. I—" Then he glanced past the man. It was Demi's apartment. There were two more men and two uniformed cops inside.

"What's all this?" Winter asked. "Where's Ms. Jeroux?"

The man closed the door behind him and confronted Winter in the corridor. "You know her?"

"I want to know what's going on."

"There's been an incident."

"Incident!"

"Your name, please."

"Winter. Rogue Winter. R-O-G-U-E. Who the hell are you? What incident?"

"Do you have any I.D. on you, Mr. Winter?"

Winter whipped out his wallet and shoved it at the man who opened and inspected it. "I'm asking you," Winter growled. "Who are you? What twigs? Where's Ms. Jeroux?"

The man returned the wallet. "She'll have to wait. Friend of hers, Mr. Winter?"

"Yes, and I—"

"Know her well?"

"What the hell business is it of yours? Who are you?"

"Dampier. Sergeant Dampier." He flashed a gold badge long enough to be read in nanoseconds.

"You're police?"

"That's right, Mr. Winter. Are you a relative of Ms. Jeroux?"

"No, and I—"

"But a close friend?"

"God damn your eyes! Where's Demi? What's happened?"

"How did you happen by this morning?"

"We had a date. We—Look, I'm not going to stand for this much longer. D'you think I'm the type that runs screaming at the sight of a cop? I want to know where Ms. Jeroux is and what's happened to her."

"You think something's happened?"

"That has to be obvious. Is she all right?"

Dampier nodded coolly, as if making up his mind. "I'm from Third District Homicide."

"Homicide!" Winter shouldered past him and shoved the apartment door open. Dampier put a restraining grip on his arm. The apartment was a shambles. Winter looked around wildly, all his famous poise gone. "What? Who? How? Where's Demi?"

"We don't know."

"You said homicide."

"That's right."

"But no body?"

"No body."

"Then why? How? What makes you think . . ." He tried to control himself. "What happened? Exactly."

"The neighbors heard screaming and crashing," Dampier said. "Violent struggle. They called us at nine-forty."

"I left here at nine," Winter muttered. "I was with Young, talking about her, and we never knew . . ."

"So it's presumed homicide, with the body removed," Dampier continued calmly. "Possibly by you, since you were intimate with her."

"Goddam you!"

"Come on, Mr. Winter. You spent the night here. Some of your gear is in the mess. Just back from Ganymede, huh? That's what the tags on your tote say. Lovers' greeting or lovers' quarrel?"

"We were planning on getting married."

"Changed your mind?"

"No, damn you."

"Did she?"

"No."

"Find her with another man?"

"What's your name? Dampier? I swear I'll—"

"Easy. Easy. You wouldn't believe how many homicides are committed by people who've been intimate. I have to know all this. It's better answering questions here than at the station."

"Gig," Winter breathed hard.

"You know this apartment well?"

"Well enough."

"Is anything missing, outside of the girl? Look around, but don't touch anything."

Winter looked at the jumble helplessly. There were thrown books on the floor, the contents of the desk, his tote, its contents, smashed decorations; it looked as though a dinosaur had run wild. "I don't know," he said at last. "I just can't tell."

"Too bad," Dampier said. "We need all possibles. Was there anything special or different about her that might give us a lead?"

Winter opened his mouth, then closed it. "Nothing special," he said at last. "Just a fine Virginia girl. And why do you use the past tense?"

"It's a pretty safe presumption that she was killed. She have any enemies?"

"None that I know of."

"Friends?"

"The only ones I know are the people who work with her in our office. There may have been others."

"What office?"

"*Solar Media.*"

"Hey!" one of the plainclothesmen said. "This must be *the* Rogue Winter. Should've known by them scars."

"Wait a minute," Winter exclaimed. He made a lightning tour of the closets, dressing room and bath. "Her cat's gone."

"Cat? What cat?"

"She had a pet; half Siamese, half koala."

A cop offered, "Probably run out, scared by the

fight and the kill."

Winter shuddered; Dampier made careful notes. "Right. I'll be in touch, Mr. Winter. The supervisor may want you for more questions. You're not planning on leaving town?"

"I'm planning on getting bombed," Winter said. He couldn't stop shaking.

Dampier looked into the ashen face. "Good idea. Numb's the name of the game for you."

o o o

There was an eager crowd in the street waiting to see whether a body would be carried out covered with a red blanket (still living) or a black (dead). Three police vans were arriving, probably containing scientists. Winter lurched through the mob (half dead) and searched out transport.

"We'll zig the Solar Circuit," he told the driver.

"Inside out or outside in?"

"Start outside."

"You got it."

So THE TRITON THUNDER was the first stop. Pagoda exterior. Teahouse interior w. teak, ebony, pearl and jade. Lanterns. Four fat mandarins (all paid-up members of Actors Equity) dancing in slow-motion postures on the center floor with snapping fans and hand-bells and singing in eunuch shrills. The drinks had names like "Elegy for a Fallen Leaf," "Vengeful Dragon," "Moon-love," and "Year of the Quark."

"One of each," Winter ordered.

Next, THE SATURN SICK-VI. Foreign Legion Fort

exterior w. cannon and the dummies of dead soldiers (Criterion Costume Co.) in the embrasures. Interior; sand, palms, trestle tables, vedette waiters. Music by Alfie Dreyfus & His Deafening Duo on accordion. Drinks; Hash, Morph, Coke, Ope, Roach I, Roach II and Roach III.

"One of each."

He brought his driver into THE CALLISTO QUEEN for protection. It was a fag joint with waiters in drag, looking and acting dangerously seductive. Tiffany glass chandeliers, stained glass windows backlighted to illuminate "The Probable Possible Postures." Music by The Rough Traders. Drinks named "Hustle," "Cruise," "Grope," "Lust Letter," "Obscene Bus Stop."

"Two of each."

Then THE GANYMEDE GENITAL, a nude trap. You check your clothes and are handed cosmetics to make up blackface or whiteface, as your choice might be. Congo decor. "Fever" drinks; Yellow, Dengue, Spotted, Breakbone, Scarlet, etc. MARS BOW BELLS, a mirrored gin palace w. aphrodisiac buffet. THE TERROR FIRMA with built-in practical jokes. THE LUNA TIC. THE VENUS ANDROGYNY for the trans-sex recuperates. THE MURK. I was waiting for him there at the black-lit bone bar decorated with bleached skulls, each with an apple in its jaws.

Shock and drink had produced an artificial massive calm to control the screaming inside him. If it cracked he would end up weeping hysterically, but I didn't think what I had to tell him would move him to tears.

"Greetings, great and good Brünehilde," he said baffably, sitting down alongside me at the empty bar. "Queen of Iceland. Wife of King Gunther. Also Wagner's Valkyrie and Siegfried's popsy." He appropriated my drink. "I see you still have my number, or was I tailed?"

"What difference does it make, Rogue?" I said. "I'm here to talk to you. I'm very, very sorry about all this."

"What's to sorrow? Love comes, love goes, but girls go on forever. If that makes any sense," he added. "Should I try it transposed?"

"Especially because part of this mess is my fault."

"Girls come, girls go, but love goes on forever. Not much of an improvement. How?" he shot.

"I held something back. *Suppressio veri*, they call it, legalwise. I had to until you were formally enthroned."

"Why?"

"Because you would have refused the throne absolutely, and we need you in that spot."

"Why?"

"It's the crux of the Meta Mafia scam."

"That Jink girl in the Bologna Dome?"

"No. She's one of the Triton ops trying to break the Mafia. The Mafia isn't an inside Chinese operation."

"But everybody thinks—"

"It's Maori, and you're now Kingfather of the scam."

He was thunderstruck.

"That's how Te Uinta was able to finance your

expensive upbringing and education.",

He was still speechless.

"And that's why your— Why this happened to Demi Jeroux. Triton will go to any lengths to break up the bootlegging, and now you're the target. They're leaning on you heavy to force you to end it."

"By wiping Demi?" He shook his head in confusion. "That doesn't make sense."

"Of course not, which is why I don't think she was killed. I think she was snatched. She'll be the price they offer. That's why I had to see you as soon as possible to plan your next—"

"You knew this and you let it happen?" he broke in. White fury replaced the drink flush and his royal sunbursts turned livid.

"I didn't know *how* it would happen."

"I told you she must be protected and you said you'd take care of it. 'Trust me,' you said."

"At least she may be alive."

"May be. You think. More of your trustable guarantees?"

"No."

"Is she alive? Yes or no."

"I don't know. I can only hope that I'm right about the Triton tactics."

"Has she been snatched? Yes or no."

"I don't know. I can't know. All we can do is wait. If they contact you, we'll know."

"And you're here to plan my next move." He snorted. "Don't look now, Mata Hari, but they can contact me, if they ever do, no matter whether Demi's alive or dead, and who's to know."

"True, but—"

"You clever bitch. You're all so smart-ass, chess game, roundabout, 'Twelve Days of Christmas' asshole clever. You can't do anything the simple, direct way. No, that wouldn't be brilliant. That wouldn't be worthy of James Bond. You have to fuck up the Solar with your dumb complications and now you've fucked me. Thanks, Odessa. Some day I'll pay you back. You'll know it's me because it'll be simple and direct."

Winter raged out of the bar and I saw him flag transport. He had himself driven to the *Beaux Arts* rotunda. He was still raging when he entered his apartment. Then his breath exploded and his wrath evaporated when he saw Demi's psycat stretched out comfortably on the couch and her key to his apartment lying on the coffee table with a flower thrust through the perforated bow.

But no Demi Jeroux.

o   o   o

"So! No snatch, no kill!" He was charged with joy. "She got away from the Jinks, came here and left me the good news, like a fine considerate Virginia girl. Said message consisting of you," he added, picking up the psycat and kissing her. "And the key." He kissed the key.

"Now, if I dig patterns, she's taken it on the lam to protect herself, and God only knows what disguise she's transformed into, like the flaky Titanian girl that she is. How in hell can I find somebody who can be anybody? You?" he asked suddenly.

He disengaged his neck from the smitten psycat.

"Demi? No fun and games now. Demi?"

"Qrst," the psycat responded, halfway between a Siamese waul and a koala churr.

"Oh, come on now, love. It's you, isn't it?"

"Rsvp," the psycat rauled melodiously.

"Always to doubt, never to know," Winter muttered. "Damnation! I've got to find our lammister but the trouble is she don't want to be found. Add a Jink hit to her pregnancy panic and the poor kid must be wild."

He settled on the couch with his feet up on the coffee table while the psycat rustled on his lap, getting comfortable.

"Shhh," he murmured. "I'm synsensing the room. Maybe something here can give me a clue."

He sensed the Anima patterns in silence, listening to prints, pictures, furniture, souvenirs, anything Demi might have touched. Some were slow and tedious, others brisk and bright, their voices like a score of superimposed, unrelated graphs:

```
JeSuisJoliJeSuisJoliJeSuisJoliJeSuisJoliJeSuis
   PINE              P            PINE
          e                  e
 A     A  tulip   A     A  tulip A     A    tulip
          e                  e
JAPAN     c      JAPAN     c    JAPAN
    TOE   t      ERR       t             TOE
          r                  r
  GII     i        GOE     i       GII
          c                  c
COE       t                      COE
          y          SUM     y
```

"Come on, friends," he coaxed. "You must have noticed my girl. She certainly paid plenty of attention to all of you our first night together. Gig? So how long was she here? When did she leave? What was she wearing?"

Nothing but more crossword patterns.

He sighed. "Egomaniacs, all of them. Never notice anything except themselves. *Le monde, c'est moi* should be their motto."

He consulted with the cat. "What's your advice, lady? Should I call Odessa Partridge? Oh sure. I can see her concocting another 'Twelve Days' brilliance. How about Dampier? Yeh. I can hear myself giving a description for Missing Persons: Color, any; height, any; weight, any; *und so weiter* . . .

"About the only thing I can be sure of is her sex, but go dig a female hippo from a male. I can just see myself picking a hippo up by the hind legs to inspect its genital *apparat*. You know, baby, I think I've got the wrong end of the pattern."

The psycat wurred and he meditated. "I have got to find her fast. So long as she's running like The Madwoman of Titania, alone, unprotected, she can't be safe. Sooner or later the Jink soldiers must catch up with her. I can't leave her on her own . . .

"The question is, has she ridden off in all directions or will she be somewhere near? My estimate is, near. Why? Consider the pattern, my dear Dr. Pusscat. Our girl is in a wild panic for herself, but also for me. She knows about the Venucci hit. And why else bring you here to reassure me about her? She loves me madly, poor sprite, and she's devoted to both of us. She could never desert. She'll be around, somewhere, somehow, trying to protect both of us, like the noble Virginia girl that she is . . .

"But hanging back and waiting is playing it Girls Rules," he growled in a sudden anger that made the cat jump. "This *crise* has got to be attacked with action, which means I've got to find her first. How? I don't go looking for her. I go out with a blank mind, thinking nothing, and wait for her to happen to me. I keep every sense open and, by God, the antipattern must force her happening."

Chapter Eight

THE SEARCH

For 'tis a truth well known to most;
That whatsoever thing is lost,
We seek it, ere it come to light,
In every cranny but the right.
                    —William Cowper

He left the *Beaux Arts* to drift aimlessly through the Jungle-Mother, at random, without design. And yet Winter's serendipity imposed an unconscious pattern on him. If you can recognize it, send in your answer and you may win one of five giant cash scholarships to the Solar School of Sleuthery.

He ran into Ching Sterne, editor and publisher of *Solar Media*, who was carefully avoiding stepping on the pavement cracks to protect his money.

"Rogella, bubie! What are you doing out, at large? You should be sweating over your hot computer. Bologna deadline, remember?"

"I'm not going to meet it, Ching."

"Oi!"

"I've got personal problems."

"Since when did you ever let a girl stand between you and a check?"

"How'd you know it was a girl?"

"A woman's the only thing that can make a man forget money."

"Any idea who she is, Ching?"

"No. The only idea I have is splitting her skull. You've never missed a deadline before, Rogue."

"She's worth it."

"No girl's worth it. Damn her, now I'll have to reschedule. Love? Pfui!" and Sterne continued toward the *Media* offices, still avoiding dangerous cracks.

Winter noticed a mule tethered before the "Forty-Mule-Team Tavern," which had been watching the encounter with stolid concentration. He went to the animal and spoke softly. "Demi? Demi?" He pulled the gold seal ring out of his pocket and displayed it. "Here's your engagement ring, Demi. State flower of Virginia. Would you like to try it on?"

No response. The mule continued gazing off at nothing. Winter made a face and was about to drift on when he saw a ranch brand on the animal's flank. It was a circle over a cross which might almost be a sunburst. He was startled and induced to enter the tavern, maybe to have a drink, and jigjeeze if there wasn't Hasty Harry bending the ear of the blonde bargirl.

Harry was a colleague, a brilliant writer who talked the greatest story in the world but—for whatever reasons—could never deliver. He lived entirely on the advances and loans he received for his persuasive proposals. Consequently he was constantly on the run from editors clamoring for their stories, and creditors hollering for their money. He was into Winter for five thousand.

"Hey Rogue—Hi Rogue—Whatchadrinkin'?" Hasty Harry's delivery was in machine-gun

bursts.   "JustbeentellinBlondiehere—Gottagreat
story—Circulatinglibrary—forbrains—Renta
brainfor anypurpose—Have it stuckinya skull—
dig—But this guy—he'sthreemonthsoverdue—
onnis rent—so theywanna repossess—"

"And you're three years overdue on my five
yards, Harry." He turned to the bargirl. "Straight
ethyl on the rocks, please." Then he noticed she
was wearing a sunburst pendant on a chain. Again
startled. "Demi?" he asked.

"Martha," she smiled as she served him.

"That fivegrandbaby," Hasty Harry said.
"Nocando—brokebustedbankrupted—But—Gotta
great offerfrom Brazil—onnascriptIsoldem—
Thisguycomesintathistown—Hassagreatbash—
Townfallsalloverhim—Moneywomenhonors—
Findsoutitsadead ghosttown—Lonely—Try'nto
keepimthere—Makemillions—OnlyIgottahire
Portugeesytranslator—"

It cost Winter another loan to learn how "The
Town That Haunted a Man" turned out.

"Poor Harry," he muttered as he left the tavern.
"All he can do is sell his stories. Why can't he ever
write 'em?"

He stopped thinking and drifted aimlessly,
senses receptive but not searching. Then he
became aware of a sound following him, a tap-tap-
tapping. He stopped and turned curiously. It was a
tall, slender figure, dressed in tatters with a ski
hood over the head and a tap-tap-tapping cane in
one hand. A sign hanging from the neck read:

DEVOID OF FACULTY
OF SPEECH & SIGHT
PLEASE HELP

There was a cup attached to the sign. The woolen ski hood had no eye or mouth openings. It was decorated with a woven Swedish design of a sunburst.

Winter waited for the beggar to tap up to him, then clanked coins into the cup and asked, "Demi?"

"Thah yuh," came the muffled reply. "Ah Bah-Bah-Rah."

"Barbara?"

"Yah. Ah Bah-Bah-Rah. Gah blah yah."

And Winter watched her tap-tap away down the jostling street, quite unaware that he was being subjected to an artful exploration by Perce the Peacock.

Perce was a dip and preposterously vain. He blew half his take on clothes; Old Scottish cashmere in winter (he always claimed that he personally shot the cashmeres) and printed silk *crêpe de chine* in summer. He wore pearl necklaces and pearl dog collars (gold or platinum metals might sound a warning with their tinklings) but, of course, nothing on his slender wrists and fingers.

Unhappily for Perce, this day he was wearing a diamond-and-sapphire wedding band which he had liberated the week before. It was so glorious that he couldn't resist the temptation to flash it, despite the fact that it was two sizes too large.

Alas, when Perce withdrew his hand with Winter's wallet, he discovered that he had left the ring behind in Winter's pocket.

Perce was appalled. He followed the ambling Winter, wondering what to do. He glanced through the wallet but didn't even bother to count the cash. To hell with it, there would always be another to lift; he wanted his beautiful ring. He snarled at a blind beggar clinking a cup, but that inspired a plan. He caught up with the drifting Winter, stopped him, and proffered the wallet.

"Scuse me, mister. This belong you? I think maybe you drop it, huh?"

Again a startle. Perce's *crêpe de chine* was printed with a sunburst pattern.

"Dem—" Then Winter stopped himself. Obviously not. He took the wallet and examined it. "Yes, this is mine, by God. How did I—? I can't thank you enough. Perhaps a reward? Name it."

"No reward, sir, but—but, well, I was look for a ring I drop, my wife's, which is how I happen to find your wallet. I—Did you maybe find a ring?"

"Sorry," Winter smiled. "I wish I could return the favor, but I didn't."

"Oh, sir, maybe you do and forget?"

"Not a chance. Sorry."

"Could happen, sir. You look absent-in-the-mind type. Maybe pick up and put in pocket without remember? You look, huh? Wife's. Diamond and sapphire. Just look, huh?"

Not very bright, really, but his hands did most of the thinking for him.

"Hi! Nig!" Winter shouted. "Wait a minute!"

Then, to Perce, "Sorry. Thanks again," and he galloped across the road to join a charming albino lady complete with dark shades for her red eyes, wide-awake hat to protect her head, and full-sleeved body sheath to guard every inch of her skin against the sun. Nigelle Englund. Winter remembered well what was being protected by that sheath.

"Doctor," he whined, "I got like holes in my head where I got kicked by a mammoth on Ganymede. Is there any hope for the mammoth?"

Nig laughed. She was a vet, analyst, specializing in the hang-ups and neuroses of the bizarre crossbred pets of the Solar, which produced some beauties. "No more Shrink City, Rogue," she said. "I am now the Den Mother."

"Who den? What den?"

"The city zoo. I'm the *Gnädige Direktor*."

"Jigjeeze! And to think I knew you when."

She gave him a look which he could feel stinging him through her dark glasses. "Let's zig it, tall, dark and handsome. The zoo is nudgering me."

Then he noticed the sunburst rims of her shades. "Demi?" he asked.

"What?"

"You researched me, Demi. Maybe you heard about me and Nig?"

"The last time, Rogue," she said in hard, level tones, "it was, '*Solar*'s sending me to Titan, love. Back in five weeks.' What's this Demi swindle now?"

"Sorry," he mumbled. "Sorry. I'm loose in the brain. Just quoting a line from a story I'm working on. Leave us take off for your animal farm, if you don't mind crazy company. God knows, I need a little aid and comfort right now."

"Not from me, loverboy. You can pour your heart out to the animals. They're a captive audience."

He cruised the natural habitats (the zoo was powerfully environment-minded); kudu, dingo, onager . . .

"Demi?"

"Demi?"

"Demi?"

No response. He stopped to watch a crowd of kids, visitors from all over the Solar, laughing, cheering and jeering at a remarkable life-size marionette show. The EcoArgument: This dirty, rotten ringmaster (HISS!) tortures animals into leaping through burning hoops, juggling, and riding contraptions, with a red-hot whip. (BOO!) Then a determined ape rebels, (CHEERS!) the other animals join the revolt, (HOORAY!) and they overpower the vicious ringmaster (LAUGHTER!) and force him to perform their antics with his own whip. (JEERS!) Music: "Carnival of the Animals."

Winter wandered on; tatousy, dziggetai, geeko . . .

"Demi?"

"Demi?"

"Demi?"

Nothing. Babirussa, colugo, bandicoot, kiang, eft, peba . . .

"Demi?"

He was only half-hoping anyway. He stopped to watch a magnificent maritime carousel; sea horses, porpoises, whales, dolphins, giant mollusks, friendly sharks, and even an obliging octopus, all ridden by kids from the Solar (plus a few unashamed adults) to the music of "La Mer," emphysema'd on the calliope. He was slightly startled to see the blind beggar mounted on the octopus, waving her cane in time to the music.

"Reminds me of the coronation joke," Winter thought and resumed his random walk. Tiger, snow leopard, giraffe, catamount, lynx, dromedary, puma, cougar; and in a veld of black panthers, one came up to the barrier and regarded him with such soulful yearning that he was almost convinced.

"Demi, it *has* to be you. Yes? Now come on out, love, I've got a reward for you. Look. Your engagement ring." He reached into a pocket and pulled out a diamond-and-sapphire wedding ring.

He hooted with laughter; he'd twigged the entire caper in a flash. "Demi, if it's really you, come out and share the joke." But the panther had turned away. Winter searched to be sure he also owned the seal ring. "There's only one thing I can't dig," he chuckled as he left the zoo, tossing the wedding band, "and I'll have to ask the little punk sometime. I suppose he has a police record. I can look him up."

There was no need. At the gate he collided with Perce and a tall, thin legal eagle, bursting in as though in hot pursuit, which indeed they were. "That's him!" Perce cried, and without

preliminary the eagle pointed the accusing talon
of a district attorney at Winter and harangued him
about stolen property, lawful pursuit, legal
search, writs of replevin, and court action with
damages.

Winter grinned and tossed the ring. "Quick
work. What's your name?" he asked the dip.

"Perce."

"Perce what?"

"Just Perce."

"Counsel claims this is your ring?"

"My wife's."

"How'd I get it? Found it?"

"You never!" Perce was indignant. "You pick
my pocket when I give back wallet."

"Do shut up, counselor," Winter advised the
ranting legal eagle. "Tell you what, Perce. Let's
drop the charges and countercharges. I'll return
the ring if you'll tell me one thing."

"What?"

"How in hell could you drop it when you were
lifting my wallet?"

Perce actually blushed. He hesitated until he
was reassured by Winter's warm glance. "Slip off.
Too big."

Winter was grateful for his second laugh in an
infuriating day. He handed Perce the ring.
"Shouldn't wear it in your line of work. Going to
rip the streets again?"

"No action," Perce confided. As usual, Winter
had made another instant friend. "Better the
carny, you think, huh?"

"Gig, Perce," Winter smiled. "Let's go."

CHIEF RAINIER'S
INDIAN CARNIVAL

Russian trained bears, Swedish gymnasts, German *Tanzsaal*, Gypsy fortune-tellers, Basque pelota, Hindu magicians, Italian *bocce*, Turkish delight, French pastry, Alaska seals, English dog races—about the only thing Indian in the carny was Chief Rainier himself who was guarding the front entrance, resplendent in war bonnet, war paint, and breechclout. The baton he used to point out the attractions was a tomahawk.

"How!" he grunted. "Where sun rise, white man's land. Where sun set, red man's land. This red man's land. Ugh! Me pay all tax. Me got all license. Red man smoke peace pipe. Why white man police come scalpum red man? Want more wampum? Ugh! No can do. Chief Rainier's tepee empty."

"But we're not the fuzz, chief," Winter said. "We're just plain paying customers."

"Gentlemen! Gentlemen! Forgive me," Chief Rainier apologized. "I've been much harassed by officials who, I'm sorry to say, come crunching for payoffs. What poet said, 'Temptation hath a music for all ears'? Come in. Enter. Box office on the left. Enjoy yourselves."

"Now that's a *good* Indian. How could you possibly rip his show?" Winter asked, but Perce was already gone about his business. "Dedicated," Winter murmured, making sure the seal ring and wallet were still with him.

He wandered, admiring clowns, contortionists,

tumblers, sword-swallowers, snake-charmers and,
particularly, an "Ecumenical Belly-Dancer" God
save the mark! The carnival catalyzed
remembered laughter of Rabelais:

The Games Of Gargantua

Then the carpet being spread, he played

At the chess.	*At blind-man-buff.*
At trump.	*At the beast.*
At nivinivinack.	*At the hardit arsepursy.*
At the tarots.	*At thrust out the harlot.*
At bumdockdousse.	*At rogue and ruffian.*

At the unlucky man.
At the unfortunate woman.
At the torture.
At the last couple in hell.

And suddenly Rabelais didn't seem so funny.
Then, alongside a hairy Bulgarian fire-eater who
was also billed as a fire-walker, he saw a tent with
a lurid banner. It displayed a smiling sun which
was unquenchably Paddyfaced and whisky-red.
Each of the twelve green flames bursting from the
sun ended in a sign of the Zodiac.

MADAME BERNADETTE—SEES ALL—KNOWS ALL

"An Irish gypsy," Winter exclaimed. "A tinker!"
He entered the tent just in time to hear a whale
cough next door and see a fireball bounce on the
tent roof and explode. He heard wild shouts.

Evidently the Bulgarian had goofed. The ancient, dry plastic flared like tinder, blasting down heat and smoke. The tinker crone was clutching her crystal ball and staring up at the inferno as though it was the wrath of God. By the time Winter got her out they were both charred and steaming, but she never let go of her crystal ball.

"You should be Aquarius," he told Madame Bernadette, "or else insured. If you're Demi, serves you right. *Are* you Demi?"

No answer. He shoved through the excited crowd, left the carnival and limped to ffunky ffreddy's ffashions, where he negotiated for an instant replacement of his wrecked clothes under a sign warning him that ffreddy was guarded against shoplifters by Vigilant Video, Inc. To drive the point home, their logo was a sun with an eye in it and a motto printed around it like a solar corona: While We Watch, You're Never In The Dark.

Ffunky ffreddy's advertised in *Solar Media* and Winter was recognized as a celebrity. They were delighted to help him clean up and fitted into new clothes. He was refreshed and grateful when he left the tailor shop, yet wrapped in a thunderous gloom over the failures of that exasperating day and furiously uncertain about how to cope with the disaster into which he and Demi had been plunged. A distant tap-tap-tapping sounded like time running out.

Then three Triton soldiers hit him.

o   o   o

Winter raged past the two apprentices in the
orchestra salon and burst into my studio where I
was struggling with the reluctant virginal, still
trying to get it up to true concert pitch. He looked
like a Cockney "Pearly King," said pearls being his
skin showing through rents in his wrecked
clothes. He was so furious that the sunbursts on
his cheeks glowed. Every inch the killer king, or a
mad bull sea lion (*Eumetopias lubeta*) in search of
his harem.

"All right, Odessa," he growled. "Your plan of
op. Let's have it."

"Sit, baby, and cool it. I think maybe you need a
drink."

"I've had enough today to launch a fleet." He
was shaking. "What's the plan?"

"Drink," I said firmly and rang. He glared. Barb
came in, carrying a tray with one hand, tap-tap-
tapping her cane with the other. That froze him.
He gaped at her, at me, and would have sank onto
nothing if I hadn't shoved a chair under his butt.

Barbara put the drink tray down and pulled off
the ski hood, revealing the head they used to
stamp on coins; "Liberty" or "Marianne." A clean-
cut dyke face (lesbians make our best *Gardas*) that
suited her lean, tough body. "Ah Bah-Bah-Rah,"
she mumbled, then, "Christ, Winter, you led me
one hell of a chase."

He was nonpulsed, as Soho Young used to say.

"Richman, poorman, beggarman, thief." She put
a brandy in his hand. "And so on. Was that

deliberate or accidental?''

"Unconscious-deliberate, Barb," I said. "Rogue really doesn't understand how he resonates to Anima Mundi patterns."

"Doctor, lawyer, Indian chief . . . " Winter nodded. "Of course. No, it wasn't deliberate. I thought I was just drifting and waiting for Demi to—" He choked on his brandy. "And something was leading me?''

"Gig, Rogue," I said. "Just the way you were led to finding that drowned child in the Welsh Dome. Soul of the World. The bottom line that lets you hear things talking and lets you see what everybody's seeing but makes you think what nobody else has. You call it synergy. I call it Anima Mundi. Same thing."

"God, maybe?''

"Some people call it that. Why not? Same thing."

He nodded again. "The whole is greater than the sum of its parts, no matter what you name it." He turned to Barb. "You were tailing me?''

"So assigned."

"You know about my Demi?''

"So briefed."

"Did I—Did she—No, wait. I'm so goddam hassled that I can't put anything straight." He took a breath. "Was there any living thing always near me, around me, staying with me, that I didn't notice?''

Barb shook her head.

"Anything try to contact me that I didn't notice?''

"Outside of Perce the Peacock, nothing but the three Jap-Chink soldiers, and you gave two of them plenty of notice before they died. Man, the Maori really know how to train killers on Ganymede. Attila the Hun could take lessons from you."

"Two? One got away?"

"No."

Winter looked at her, then at me. I shrugged. "You were pretty busy taking two, so Barb lent a hand. She's a dead shot at fifty yards. Hope you don't mind."

"I'm not that much of a macho pig. I'm grateful, Barb, damned grateful. Thanks."

"Us guys got to stick together," Barb grinned.

"Thanks again. Now look, stand by me still, both of you. I've got to bring my girl back to me before anything else, and I'm licked. I never thought the day would come when I couldn't piece patterns together when I was under the gun with so much at— Never mind. Suggestions?"

"You've got to make a deal with Triton," I said.

"Go ahead."

"They want the smuggling and bootlegging stopped."

"Can't handle it themselves?"

"No. You're the only one who can, King R-og."

"I don't want to." He began to anger again. "Those cocked-up Jinks, sitting on their Meta, humiliating the Solar, like those old goddam Arabs, sitting on their oil . . . "

"And the rest of the Solar agrees with you, particularly since Triton has started buying us up with their Meta money . . . this *Paire Banque* building belongs to them . . . but do you want your Demi back?"

"Dear God! What a question! Why d'you think I've been making a damned fool of myself all day?"

"Then you'll have to pay the price. She won't return until she's assured that the heat's off."

He grunted.

"And the price is ending the Maori Mafia."

He waved an impatient hand. "Suppose I do. What guarantees do I get that'll reassure her, wherever she is?"

"Ah! That's where we bargain. We ask for written guarantees, which aren't worth a damn. We ask for fines in escrow, and they couldn't care less. They probably own any bank it's deposited with. We—"

"Wait a minute. When and where does this take place?"

"When and where they approach you."

"And what'll make them approach me?"

"Why, you're going to apply for a visa to visit the Celestial satellite. That shows you're ready to do business, and they'll take it from there."

He gave Barb a wry glance. "Tinker, tailor, soldier, sailor," he said. "So I'm the finish of the jingle, sailing off to Triton. I tell you, this Anima Mundi is a race apart." Back to me. "Then what do you really ask for?"

"Nothing. After the traditional negotiation ballet we spring one hard fact on them."

"What?"

"That we've got a hostage in escrow."

"No! Who?"

"The highest-ranking mandarin in the Triton directorate. Their information and decision shogun. Head of 'The Fists of Righteous Harmony,' once 'The Boxer Tong' back in the nineteenth century."

"You've got that *macher?* Here on Terra?"

"Not exactly. We've I.D.'d him, a distinguished researcher . . . Tomas Young."

He was flabbergasted.

"Ta-mo Yung-kung on Triton. The 'kung' radical signifies 'duke.' He's a Manchu nobleman."

"The great exobiologist?"

"You got it."

"The friend who said he'd be honored to examine and advise my Demi?"

"Would have saved them a lot of trouble."

"B-but— But how?"

"Ancillary covers, Rogue. That's S.O.P. in Intelligence. I met Tomas as Soho Young, running a hockshop in the Jungle years ago. Ever hear of a hard-porn pleasance called *'Bedbeat'?"*

"Him, too?"

"No, me."

"My God! How do you clowns play all these different roles?"

"Don't you play different roles when you're inquisiting and synergizing?"

"We're way past the age of simplistic survival," Barbara put in. "That's what wiped the dinosaurs. Today it's: The Multi Shall Inherit the Earth."

"Cloak-and-dagger kid stuff," Winter scoffed.

"No, hard-boiled accounting," I said wearily. "A question of time and budget. We all know there are Intelligence agents operating; we take that for granted. The problem is how to keep *your* agents working as long as possible before *their* Counterintelligence catches up. Dig?"

"Gig."

"So you set up a fake ring as a decoy ring. The fakes don't know it; they think they're the only real thing. You hope that Counter will squander its budget on the expendable decoys while the professional ring works behind them, but you have to direct the phonies to keep them from blundering near the realsies. That's what Young was doing from his hockshop. That's what I'm doing from *'Bedbeat.'*"

"I will be damned," Winter muttered.

"Now look, I made a mistake last time. I didn't give you credit for being as bright and hip as you seemed to be, and I apologize. My only excuse is the second law of Intelligence: Nobody's as smart as they seem."

"What's the first?" he growled.

"That *we're* not as smart as we think. So I'm going to level with you."

"Should you?" Barbara asked quietly.

"I have to, Barb," I said. "First, apply for a Triton visa. Two: jet to Ganymede and stop the Mafia operation. This is a must because I'll tell you what's really at stake."

"Tell," he snapped.

"Let Triton keep their Meta monopoly. We can go on paying through the nose a little while longer, but we've got to stop their buying spree and take-over of the Solar right now. In fifty years they'll own us."

"So you're going to hang back and bargain?"

"Once your Mafia is cooled and you and your girl are safe, we've got Ta-mo Yung-kung as our ace in the hole and a winning hand at best. If it turns into a Mexican standoff, at least it gives us time to work something else out."

He flew into a murderous macho rage. "You and your asshole girly-girly ploys! Bargains! Trade-offs! Standoffs! Can't you understand you're deal-ing with grown men who don't play games? We fuck you and dump you and good luck to your goddam delusions. You think you've got me as a card to play?"

"Rogue!"

"I'll tell you what you've got, a Maori double-kill king."

"For God's sake, man . . . "

"Oh, I'll go through your motions, but when I get to Ganymede it won't be to end the Mafia-bit; they'd only laugh at me. Anybody but a goddam woman could call that. No. I'll order a hit and every Maori soldier will cheer. D'you understand me, Brünnehilde? You've got a Mafia contract on Triton."

He'd made his decision and shot out of the studio. I looked at Barb, not pleased with the development and even less with myself. "Maybe I should have listened to you."

"He's a hopeless M.C.P. Won't we ever develop partheno-survival?" she asked. "If the aphids can do it, why can't we?''

"Stay with him, *Garda*. Want backup?''

"Negatory," she grinned, then, "and I thought it might be cute to offer him half the take from my beggar's cup!''

Chapter Nine

STRATEGY V. TACTICS

Strategems ever were allowed in love and
war.
      —Susannah Centlivre

Those oft are tactics which errors seem.
      —Alexander Pope

With 20-20 hindsight, which you're always decrying, Odessa, this is how I see the gigs and goofs of what I did after I tore out of your office in a flaming rage. I'd yelled about a contract on Triton. Christ Almighty! I was burning to take a contract on the whole Solar if that was the cost of getting my Demi back. Where was she? Where was she holed up? How was she? Was she safe? I didn't have a clue. It shaped up like a fight with no finish in sight.

I went back to the *Beaux Arts* rotunda, changed into featherweight jumpsuit, packed a travel tote with more light stuff—you're only allowed two hundred pounds max. per passenger, bod *and* baggage—tied a polka-dot bandanna around the psycat's neck to keep her distracted, and *schlepped* her to Nig Englund's office in the zoo.

"Animal hospital's down the street," Nig said.

"She isn't sick."

"Then why's her neck bandaged?".

"It's entertainment. She likes spots."

Nig looked at my travel gear. "Going places?"

"Uh-huh."

"And you're presenting your pet to the zoo. Listen, Rogue, we've had it with dumped household livestock. They come in with ohmhounds, wombears, zeebats, okapikes, and—"

"I want to board her with you."

"Oh? Why not a pet farm?"

"You're the only one I trust, Nig. This cat's extra-special. I don't want to take any chances on her picking up some kind of crud in a commercial boardinghouse."

"Why is she special?"

"Fifth amendment."

"Indeed. What's her name?"

"Jer—" I started and cut it off just in time. I was going to give Demi's last name and then realized that Nig meant the psycat's, which I didn't know. "She doesn't have one," I lied. "I just call her 'Madame.'"

Nig could always see through me, but this time she let it pass with, "I'll see if we have any room."

She punched the computer keyboard on her desk and the screen flashed, "½ O.K."

"I don't want Madame to share a cage," I said. "She might get hurt in a fight with her cellmate. Can't she be alone?"

"We'll try again," Nig said. "Sometimes tanks answer questions that haven't been asked." She punched more keys and this time was directed to Zone 3, House 2, Cage 7. "Right. Your ladyfriend can go in solitary with the sprag-bunnies. What does she eat?"

"Anything with spots; caviar, red and black, or—"

"She'll get black-eye-pea and pinto-bean mush and like it. When are you coming back?"

"I don't know."

"No matter. Tell Miz Jeroux she can pick the cat up anytime, provided she pays the bill."

On that shaft I got the hell out. Damn! How gossip gets around!

Thence to one of my banks—I use three in hope of outsmarting the tax pattern—for a certified bill of exchange for two thousand. Two thousand, even in paper money, *weighs*, and I was already uncomfortably close to the two hundred pounds max. A few ounces might make an awkward difference.

I wanted the bill on the embossed parchment of Orb & Co., which is so haughty and superior—they even mint their own fifty sovereign goldpieces—that the entire Solar knows and kowtows to their paper which is the despair of forgers.

To give you some idea of their uppitydom, I once cashed a check and when I got outside the bank I discovered that I'd been given a hundred too much through some mysterious mistake, human or machine. Me, the honest turkey, I went back and tried to return the extra money, and the elegant teller informed me that, "No adjustments are made by Orb after the client leaves the window, sir."

So I presented myself and requested a "fractionating" bill of exchange. That's the kind that can be honored in portions until the whole is used up. The teller (not the same one) punched the accounts keyboard and damn if the credit screen didn't flash, "½ O.K." Obviously I'd lost track of how much was stashed in each of my banks, a promising omen; if I couldn't unscramble the patterns of my loot, maybe the IRS couldn't either. I settled for the thousand; it would be enough to carry me.

I took your advice, Odessa, and went to the Triton consulate to apply for a visit visa and so indicate that I was ready to make a deal for Demi. The Jink in the office was more Jap than Chink, absurdly courteous, smiling and hissing. They don't hiss out, using the tongue, "Hsss . . ." they hiss in, drawing a breath over the lower lip, "Hfff . . ."

"Are most honor, Sieurore Hiver. (That's "Mr. Winter" in Solaranto, the Solar lingua franca.) Hfff. Such celebrate gentleman care to visit humble, faraway world. Hfff. When honor Triton with visit?"

"Sometime in the next two months."

"So." He keyed the hot line that connected the consulate with the embassy and the reply flashed back, "½ O.K." He was overwhelmed. "You are granted full six month, half year, Sieurore Hiver. Hfff. Highest possible honor. Hfff."

All smooth and sweet, but if my fury needed fresh fuel it was piled on as I left with my Triton-validated passport. Scholars know the antiquated "agenbite of inwit," the relentless gnawing of conscience. What about the agenbite of talion, the relentless passion for retaliation, for an eye for an eye? The consulate lobby was decorated with primitive art and artifacts. And there, in a beautiful frame, was stretched a skin, a Maori face, an arresting mask of ceremonial scars and sacred tattoos. It was my adoptive father, Te Uinta.

Yes, sweet talion. Yes!

So.

A *Sternreise Kompanie* ship was scheduled for liftoff for Ganymede that afternoon. It was booked solid with the exception of a cabin that was half-okay, which meant I'd have to share it with a stranger. Who? How the hell did you finagle it, Odessa? Your dyke *Garda*, Barbara Bull.

(Simple, Rogue. We booked the full cabin and held half-open. We figured it was six-two-and-even that you'd take off for Ganymede soonest. Barb could always jump ship if you didn't show.)

I like the lady a lot and am certainly beholden to her, but I didn't want to spend too much time with Barb. You people are so sharp that I was afraid I'd drop a clue to my future plans. This was a luxury jet featuring the *haute cuisine*, so I spent most of the trip in the galley, pretending I had an assignment from *Media* to interview a Null-G chef. Matter of fact, it was quite interesting, would make a grabby feature, and helped take my mind off my headaches.

Cooking in free-fall is unique. The chef floats in the middle of his kitchen which surrounds him, top, bottom, and sides. (He has to be alerted before the ship accelerates or decelerates so he can batten everything down.) He can stand on his head, as it were, and crack eggs over his shoulder. One problem is that nothing ever pours or drops or spills in free-fall; everything has to be shaken, pushed, nudged, and coaxed into position. Visualize trying to flip a flapjack in Null-G.

He has another problem. His refrigerators are cooled by the zero shadowside of the ship, with heat-boosters if they get too cold, but occasionally a craft will roll in flight exposing them to the blistering sunside. Then he picks up the intercom and berates the flight deck which hates to use the lateral jets because it wastes fuel for no good reason. "Imbeciles! You are sabotaging my *créme brûlée!* No good reason? *Étoilevoyage Compagnie* will hear of this!"

It's a delight to watch him roast meats and fowl. He positions the roast at an exact height above the electric grill and gives it a slight turn. It hangs there, revolving slowly in a free-fall barbecue. If it shifts, a gentle touch will reposition it to the chef's satisfaction, but he's painfully particular. Sometimes space-chefs get into hot arguments about RPMs and elevation in centimeters above the grill.

His French-fried shrimp are mesmeric. He shakes a container of the best oil above the grill, producing a shower of droplets. He pats them toward each other until he has a golden globe of oil coming to a sizzle. At the right moment the seasonings go in (I was never permitted to see that), followed by the shrimp, and you're transfixed by the vision of a delicious, revolving seafood balloon. It's like the sick tsarevitch being hypnotized by Rasputin's watch, only you can't eat a watch.

*In Turkish Domes the poppies grow
Between the hemp plants, row on row.*

I shook Barbara after the Ganymede landing by
leaving my gear in the cabin and slipping out
alongside my friend, the chef, wearing his soiled
uniform and high chef's hat. He, of course, was all
gussied up for the three-day layover and his Creole
girlfriends for whom I helped him smuggle in
three dozen ampules of ginseng. I insist on
repaying favors. I took a ganyfoil to the Turkish
Domes and barged in on Ahmet Tröyj to propose a
war strategy.

Ahmet's the Number One, the *gantze macher* of
the Turks. He owes me heavy, we both know it,
and I'd better explain. He's great in his office, a
brilliant bey, an artful governor who's put the
Turks into a position almost as powerful as the
Jinks; but if what I know ever got out, he'd be
impeached, epaulets torn off, sword broken over
his head, dismissed in disgrace, and —worse than
disgraced—a laughingstock. At least that's what
we tell each other.

Because years ago when I was doing a full
feature on his father, the distinguished Tröyj
Caliph, (this was long before his strange, sad
death) ambassador to a dozen capitols, papa Tröyj
decided he needed new lens transplants for his
eyes. Off he went to the chirurgeon with his son,
Ahmet, for company, and me tagging along hoping
to pick up intimate background color. Ahmet was
maybe sixteen at the time. In the chirurgery papa
thought they might as well check his son's eyes,

too. They sat Ahmet down before an eyechart and discovered that he was eagle-eyed, but didn't know how to read.

Fact. He'd been *schlepped* around the diplomatic circuit all his life, picking up sophistication, charm, and expensive tastes, having a glorious time, and it never occurred to the ambassador's entourage that Ahmet wasn't getting any basic training in the three Rs. They all took that for granted and nobody bothered to check.

Naturally Ahmet never snitched on himself; what kid wants to go to school? By the time he was sixteen it was too late for readin', writin' and 'rithmetic. To this day he can't read or write. Years of concealing his illiteracy have developed a hundred clever ruses and a fantastic memory. Fortunately for the governor they use voice prints for signatures in the Turkish enclave.

> *Can you heel, can you toe?*
> *Can you help your sister sew?*
> *Can you read, can you write?*
> *Can you help your brother fight?*

Ahmet gave me a huge hello, not because I've got the goods on him but because we really are friendly. He's in his late twenties now; chic, suave, swarthy, already balding, and stammering slightly because Terran English is his third or fourth language and sometimes he has to hesitate while he gropes for a word. I won't reproduce the stammer.

"Ahmet, I've come to beg a favor," I said, presenting him with a ginseng ampule I'd begged from the chef.

"*Faire des demandes,*" he grinned. "Go ahead. Twist my arm. I defy you. I'm prepared."

"You are?"

"A. B. C. D. E. F. G. How's that?"

"Ahmet! Ahmet! Is this any way to treat your friendly neighborhood blackmailer? You've been studying behind my back."

"It's one of your Maori numbers. She blew in out of nowhere last month. Teaches me in bed. Uses her scallop shells for the alphabet."

"Scallop shells!"

"Silver. Wears 'em as a *ceinture* around her hips. How d'you say *ceinture* in your rotten Yank? Oh yes, girdle. They go jingle-jangle-jingle when— She's got one hell of a hickey on her ass. *Tukhas? Derriere?* Ass. What's the favor, Rogue?"

"What's your Meta scam, Ahmet?"

"Simple. We pay the Jinks with skag and horse. Pound for ounce."

"Jigjeeze! Sixteen for one?"

"But at least we've got a counterthreat. They don't dare cut our Meta allotment. If they do, we cut their happy-dust shipment."

"What's your allotment?"

"Three-four hundred ounces of Meta a month."

"That much?"

"Hemp and poppies eat heat and humidity like there's no tomorrow."

"And you ship them five-six thousand pounds of dope. Refined?"

"No, crude. The Jinks prefer to purify it themselves."

"It's still a hell of a lot of junk."

"It's a hell of a lot of people. 'Pepper, salt, mustard, cider; *combien peuple* live in China?' I'm pretty sure they use a lot of the crude to keep the coolies happy in the mines. From all reports it's hell down there."

"I've never seen natural Meta, Ahmet. May I see some of yours?"

"Is this the favor?"

"Not yet."

"You use it. Why haven't you ever seen it?"

"How many people who use silver have ever seen the natural ore?"

"*Sans réplique*, as ever, Rogue. Come on."

At a side-lock we got into vacsuits so heavily insulated that they made us look and move like spastic polar bears. Ahmet tapped my helmet and pointed to the shortwave antenna. "Are you switched on? Do you read me, Rogue?"

"Loud and clear."

"Then do exactly what I tell you, and for God's sake don't touch anything, unless you want to generate yourself into a nova."

"No thanks. I've got too much burn inside me as it is."

Out into the lunar terrain and still feeling like a polar bear hopping from ice floe to ice floe, only this was from crag over crevice to rock. About a quarter of a mile out, Ahmet stopped at what seemed to be a natural tufa carapace, and deafened me over the shortwave hollering in

Turkish, not one of my languages. The carapace slid aside eventually, revealing a hatchway and stone steps leading down. We descended into a small vault with a stone door at the far side, guarded by four armed polar bears.

More jabbering in Turkish. The guards swung open the stone door which was on pivots, and we went through. The door closed behind us. "Tight security," Ahmet told me. "Not because Meta's *précieux;* because it's *dangereux.* Can't have civilians playing with these matches."

We were in a spherical ice cave. "Cryogenic helium," Ahmet explained, "in the solid crystal state. Inert, like argon and neon, only more so. It's just about the only *Substanz* that can't be catalyzed by Meta. It's used for shipping and storage containers, but it isn't easy maintaining a temperature of two degrees Kelvin."

"Ahmet, you and your Maori popsie have been reading up on the subject," I said, looking around. "What's that pile of jewelry doing here? *Précieux* goodies to protect from a rip?"

"My dear Rogue, that's your Meta."

"What! Those opal buttons?"

"Aber natürlich."

I took a step for a closer look, wondering whether this Playboy of the Solar World was indeed zigging me on. They appear to be tiny iridescent buttons, round, rimmed, shallow-domed on both sides, but not perforated. The opalescent fire in them was live, sparkling and dancing.

"This is really Meta? Seriously, now, Ahmet; no fun and games. Meta?"

"*Oui.*"

"It's beautiful."

"*Oui.*"

"But these jewels look so harmless."

"Actually they are, in the normal state. I'm being quite serious now, Rogue. They're tektites, extragalactic meteorites from deep space. You can still find ordinary tektites on Terra; black glassy buttons just lying around, harmless, minding their own business."

"Then what made these so different?"

"Ah! These are primal numbers out of the cosmic past. It's theorized that a shower of tektites, shot from elsewhen, saturated Triton during its volcanic era. They were subjected to titanic thermal and radioactive pressures and transformed into Meta. Each of these buttons is a cauldron of compressed transformation energy."

"They look it, by God!"

"That's what enables Meta to kick atoms into a quantum jump and release energy. When they lapse back to their normal level they absorb the lost radiation quanta from the Meta and jump again. All this at 'c' speed. De Broglie must be spinning in his grave."

"Who de Broglie? What de Broglie?"

"Louis Victor. He perpetrated the quantum mechanics caper back in 1923, and never knew what it would lead to."

"Ahmet Tröyj, Ahmet Tröyj, you *have* been reading up."

"The genesis is just speculation, Rogue, but it's known that Meta is found in prehistoric lava, rather like African diamonds which are found in ancient volcanic 'pipes' or necks. The Jink coolies have to mine it the same way the African Blacks used to."

"How's the stuff handled?"

"Tools with solid helium tips. Think of a blacksmith handling white-hot iron, then reverse it and you've got a whitesmith handling Meta."

"I will be damned. Thanks for the guided tour, Ahmet. I really am grateful and I won't even beg for one teentsy-weentsy tektite as a souvenir."

"Couldn't carry it anyway."

"Yeh. No pockets in these suits."

"Is this the favor, the whole *faveur*, and nothing but *di toyve*?"

"No. To tell the truth, I came here with a strategic idea, but you've given me a better tactical one. Come back to your office and I'll synergize the scam you've inspired. I want you to build me a Tröyjan Horse."

o   o   o

Of course our *TerraGardai* section had Perted the Meta Mafia operation. Here's the empiric flow chart of the trading. See if you can spot the joker in the Critical Path. No reward.

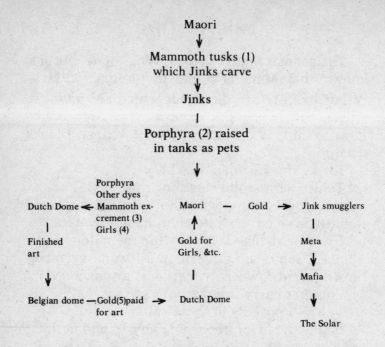

Maori
↓
Mammoth tusks (1)
which Jinks carve
↓
Jinks
|
Porphyra (2) raised
in tanks as pets
↓

Porphyra
Other dyes
Dutch Dome ◄─ Mammoth ex-   Maori — Gold ➔ Jink smugglers
| crement (3) |
Finished   Girls (4)   Gold for   Meta
art   Girls, &tc.   ↓
                                          | Mafia
↓ | ↓
Belgian dome —Gold(5)paid ➔ Dutch Dome   The Solar
                    for art

(1) The Maori hunt them with modern weapons.

(2) The shellfish that produce Imperial Purple. The Maori
pretend they use the dye for tattooing.

(3) The only organic substance which can produce a bright
green color in fireworks; also a Callisto art form.

(4) A sort of voluntary slavery. The Maori girls make lovely
and most obliging models, and anything to get away
from that damn macho Dome.

(5) The rare pink gold which the Belgians refuse to sell to the
Solar.

And have you spotted the joker?
How the hell do you heist something that can't
be touched?

In the 20th-century African mines, diamond theft by workers was a constant problem. The shifts had to submit to an exhaustive medical examination when they came up from the Blue Ground depths, and yet a few still managed to get away with raw stones. Five or ten carats of the rough, and a Black was set up for life; land, cattle, wives, luxury by native standards.

No such problem on Triton. After a cursory physical search of the shifts coming out of the lava deposits, they passed the coolies, one by one, through a thermal chamber. If the probes registered a temperature below zero centigrade they knew the dreamer was carrying some sort of concealed subzero container, and zap! And yet— And yet— Damn it! Meta *was* being stolen from the mines. How?

Diamond stones can be held in the mouth or swallowed; thrust into ears, up nostrils or the anus; hidden in the hair; very small stones can be concealed under eyelids; deliberate wounds can be slashed in the skin and diamonds implanted; u.s.w., but never with Meta. That compressed cauldron would turn the bod into a slow burning at the stake which would make an *auto-da-fé* seem pleasant by comparison.

When you Pert an operation, the weak joint in the Critical Path is called the Negative Slack. That joker was our Negative Slack, and we couldn't puzzle it out. It wasn't any comfort to us that Jinks couldn't either. But the Synergist did. He was headed from A. to B. and he stumbled on X. Good old reliable serendipity, it never lets you down.

Chapter Ten

HUNTER V. HUNTED

Hou hsi 'cheng 'chien pen. "They have a
thousand monkey-tricks."
—Ancient Chinese proverb

When Ahmet Tröyj's merry men had costumed the Maori, tested the props, and sprayed the jet into a lurid totem pole with CHIEF RANIER'S INDIAN CARNIVAL—#2 TOURING COMPANY emblazoned on the flanks in P. T. Barnum caps, they jig—after wishing Winter and *his* merry men good luck on an impossible mission—jagged back to their skag and horse farms.

Winter reviewed his cast; clowns, tumblers, acrobats, wrestlers, ring-shouters, sword-fighters, Hindu magician, one snake-charmer (played by Barbara, who'd gone to the Maori Dome for a consultation with Jay Yael after Winter gave her the slip) plus boa constrictors (loan from the Brazil Dome) stoned out of their skulls with amatol, and one Egyptian mummy contortionist. A contorting mummy! Would you believe it?

Also a non-Ecumenical belly-dancer played by the zapette who'd tired of Ahmet's ABCs—Winter was growing rather fond of this obliging teeny-zapper—a hairy fire-eater, and a three-thousand-year-old "Wandering Jew" offering the advice of the ages for a modest quarter-Syce.

(I'd best interject here, me, Odessa, because Jink money was crucial to Winter's wild chase. The Solar uses paper money, of course; banknotes, drafts, bills of exchange, &tc., but hard cash is used for small transactions. Triton uses the "Syce," short for the Sycee silver ingot. Sycee is from *sai-see*, meaning "fine silk," because the silver is so pure that it can be drawn out like silk threads when it's molten. It's shaped like the sole of a shoe, which is not unusual. The Solar worlds cling to traditional ingot shapes; gold in rings, copper in flat, round cakes, double-ax shape for bronze, tin in bars.

The Sycee or Syce ingot (symbol, SS) = approximately $20 Terran.

The half Syce, S, = $10 Terran.

The half of a half Syce, ½S, = $5.

The half of a half of a half Syce, ¼S, (that's how the complicated Jink mind operates) = $1.

I've Englished the Jink currency for you. Actually, SS, the Sycee is *yüan-pao*, the half Syce, S, is *liang fen-chih yüan-pao*, and most typically Jink, silver coins less than ¼S in value, the equivalent of Terrain nickels and dimes, are called *i-mao-ta-yang* or "Big Money." All the coins from the full Syce ingot down to the Big Money are shoe-shaped.)

Back to the #2 company of the carnival. Rogue Winter was in the role of Chief Ranier himself, resplendent in war bonnet and breechclout, with spectacular war paint masking the telltale sunbursts scarred on his cheeks.

"Now we're going to perform exactly as

rehearsed," he told the company. "Nobody takes the initiative. Nobody zags off on a promising lead. You do exactly what I tell you, no more, no less. I make the decisions. You follow orders. Above all else, we do not speak word one . . . repeat, *not word one in Maori*. Understood?"

They nodded obediently, even the tough, independent Maori soldiers who make up half the company. After all, he *was* their double-kill King R-og. He was speaking a mish-mash of Terran English, Polynesian, and Solaranto, the lingua franca of all the Solar worlds, which sounds like this: *Sieurore Hiver, avant nach oifigg eolais, favor.* (Mr. Winter, please come to the information desk.) It's not exactly the ethereal "Music of the Spheres," so you'll have to settle for translations.

There are scores of principal Domes on Triton occupied by the pure lines and blends of Japanese, Chinese, Korean, Malayan, Philippine, Annamese, and even descendants of the Cuban Chinese who still speak *Ku-Pa-Kuo*, an odd Asiatic-Spanish. The capitol of Triton is called the Cathay Dome by the rest of the Solar. The Jinks insist on calling it Chung-kuo which, if you please, means all China itself, and you'd better believe it.

As has been pointed out before, they're not famed for modesty, and Chung-kuo also stands for "The Middle Kingdom." This from the Jink tradition that Cathay is situated in the middle of a square solar system which it rules by divine decree. Triton is surrounded by four spaces to protect its purity, and beyond them lie islands like *huo-hsing* (Mars), *yüeh-liang* (Luna), and so forth which are inhabited by the savage barbarians who are rarely permitted to visit and sully the Heavenly Kingdom.

Since Triton is a blending in various proportions, its first spoken language is Jih-pen-chung-kuo, Japanese-Chinese, or Jink. Here are some social aspects of Triton, taken at random from the files which our agents are required to study in order to avoid a *faux pas* when dealing with Jinks. It will give you some idea of how archaic their feudal structure is.

The Jinks, who are the soberest people in the Solar, think it complimentary to get pleasantly drunk on festive occasions. People who are physically unable to do so often use substitutes to do it for them. Mandarins who are obliged to drink with all guests employ a sort of "Big Foot" who solemnly makes the rounds until the last guest has collapsed.

The Jinks distinguish between five kinds of drunkenness. According to them, wine flows to the:

Heart—	Producing maudlin emotions
Liver—	Producing pugnacity
Stomach—	Producing drowsiness and flushed face
Lungs—	Producing hilarity
Kidneys—	Producing desire

A bride and groom drink wine together out of cups joined by red string. Red is the lucky color, emblematic of prosperity and joy. All letters, dispatches and documents invariably have something red about them.

However, the Jinks believe that each man is so constituted by nature that he's able to absorb only a given quantity of luck. More than your quota will recoil on your head and do you harm. Frequently when the Jinks feel they've received their quota they'll give away the benefits of further good fortune.

And on the subject of marriage *a la* Triton, a husband has the right to kill his adulterous wife but he must kill her lover also; it's a case of all or nothing. Otherwise he lays himself open to prosecution for murder. It's a principle of Jink jurisprudence that no sentence can be passed until the prisoner has confessed his guilt, and there have been some lurid "confession" stories concocted.

Volumes have been written by Jink doctors on the pulse which is considered of enormous importance in diagnosis. They claim to distinguish twenty-four different kinds and make a point of taking the pulse of both wrists.

Now a Jink man may never touch a woman (of his class or above) and many philosophic treatises have been written on the problem of whether a man should rescue a drowning woman if it involved touching her. Of course doctors are forbidden, in the name of propriety, to touch their female patients, much less see them naked.

Consequently, doctors on house calls bring a small statue of a woman's naked body with them. This is passed into the patient's curtained bed-chamber with instructions how to mark the trouble spots. The statue is then handed back and the doctor makes his diagnosis on the basis of the markings.

Triton entertains curious superstitions which they take very seriously. They believe that wicked people are struck and killed by the God of Thunder for secret crimes. The lightning that usually accompanies thunder is an arrangement of mirrors by which the god can see his victim. All this on Terra, you understand, the only habited planet which has thunder and lightning. The Jinks are convinced that all Terrans are monstrously wicked and keep the god pretty busy.

Paper men and paper animals are a great source of dread on Triton. They believe that magicians can cut figures out of paper, slip them under doors or through windows, and then bring them to life to obey their iniquitous orders.

The "Mirror and Listen" mystery is used to solve perplexing problems. Wrap an old mirror in a cloth and then, no one being present, bow seven times toward the Spirit of the Hearth. Then the first words heard spoken by anyone will give a clue to the solution of the problem.

Another method is to close the eyes and take seven steps. Open eyes at the seventh and the first object seen in the mirror held in the hand will give some hint, along with the first words heard spoken. This is used in the attempt to keep a step ahead of fate, which the Jinks believe is liable to be altered without notice at the whim of heaven.

Heaven or paradise is *t'ien-t'ang*, which is also

metonymy on Triton for valuables. "To be poor in
t'ien-t'ang" means to have only a few jewels,
ornaments, and only a few valuable pieces of
clothing. This is only used by upper-class women
who never appear in public without full makeup
and expensive costume. Slave girls, lower-class
women and old women don't even try.

All overlords and underlings are unpaid on
Triton and make what they can out of their
position. In most Domes the various official
warrants and subpoenas are distributed to
runners who squeeze the victims handed over to
them. For a small bribe they will go back and
report "Nobody home." For a larger bribe they
will report "Has absconded," and so on. Jailors
take bribes to allow prisoners to remain at large
until wanted. Clerks of the court take bribes to use
their influence. All servants share equally in tips.

Government officials holding posts from the
highest to the lowest are entitled to a nominal but
actually a totally inadequate salary, but none of
them ever takes the money; they all live by what
they can gouge out of their office. It's customary
to refuse acceptance of the salary on such humble
grounds as "Want of Merit" or "Unworthy" and to
refund it to the Imperial treasury.

The stately accompaniments for these high
unpaid officials are gongs, red umbrellas, and
lackeys carrying a huge wooden fan and boards on
which the official's titles are inscribed in large
letters. Collateral branches of the Imperial family
wear a red sash as a distinction.

The everyday colloquial language of Triton is

the Japanese-Chinese Jink. All schoolchildren are required to master Jink as their first language, no matter what particular mother tongue or dialect is spoken in their home Dome. Sometimes the home speech is so different that Jink has to be taught as a foreign language.

The formal classic tongue is pure Japanese and is used only by scholars and dignitaries, although many Jinks will drop a classic word now and then to show that they've had an expensive education; e.g., the Japanese *Koe* rather than the Jink *Sei* for "voice" or *Toshi* instead of *Nen* for "year." This creates a good deal of hostility, somewhat like that of the English toward William the Conqueror and his successors who only spoke Norman French.

Winter had a smattering of Jink but didn't bother with it. He'd drafted Oparo for the role of the "Wandering Jew" because Oparo was the chief of the Maori Mafia and fluent in Jink. He would act as interpreter. Instead, when he and Oparo were admitted through the Cathay main lock, to the office of a magnificent official wearing crimson robes over steel armor, he launched into a vaudeville act, waving a toy tomahawk, war dancing and singing a gibberish song from his school years:

"We'll hang Jeff Davis from a sour apple tree.
Down went McGinty to the bottom of the sea.
She's my Annie and I'm her Joe,
So listen to my tale of WOE!
ANY ICE TODAY, LADY?
NO!
GIDDYAP!"

Rack 'em up, sack 'em up, any old time.
Match to the gas tank.
BOOM! BOOM!''

The official stared, then turned to an aide. "T'a
shuo shen-ma yang-ti hua?" (What kind of
language is that one speaking?)

Winter motioned to Oparo, who stepped
forward and delivered the tso-i formal bow to
one's superior; right fist clasped in left hand, deep
bow, and clasped hands brought up to the nose
twice. The following will give you some idea of the
Jink way of doing business.

OPARO: Tsen-ma ch'eng-hu t'a-ti chih-jen? (By
what title does one address you?)

CAPTAIN: Shang-wei men-k'ou. (I am Captain of
the main gate.)

OPARO: Lao-chia. (Thank you.)

CAPTAIN: Shih. Chao shui? (Yes. Now what do
you want?)

OPARO: P'an-wang che shih yu wan-man-chieh-
kuo. (Only the hope that our business will have a
most happy conclusion.)

CAPTAIN: Ch'ing-pien. (Be at ease.)

OPARO: Lao-chia. (Thank you.)

CAPTAIN: Pu-hsieh. (You are welcome.)

OPARO: I-ke pa-chang p'ai-pu hsiang. (It takes two
to make a quarrel.)

CAPTAIN: Chih-li pao-pu-chu huo. (Fire cannot be
bound up in a paper.)

ORARO: Kuei-ti pu kuei, chien-ti pu chien.
(Expensive things may often be cheap and cheap
things expensive.)

CAPTAIN: Pu p'a man, chih p'a chan. (Don't fear

progressing slowly, but beware of stopping.)

OPARO: She-mien. Mei-shu-shih. (Pardon us. We are humble actors.)

CAPTAIN: Chih jen, chih mien, pu chih hsin. (Knowing what a man is, is not knowing what is in his heart.)

OPARO: [Offering slug of pink gold with cupped hands] Erh t'ing shih hsü, yen chien shih shih. (What the ear hears may be false, what the eye sees are facts.)

CAPTAIN: Ah! [Hefting weight of gold in palm] Pu-kan-tang. (I cannot dare assume your courtesy is deserved by myself.)

OPARO: Ni t'ai ch'ien-la, Shang-wei. (You are too modest, Captain.)

CAPTAIN: Kuei-ch'u? (From what honored place do you come?)

OPARO: Ti-ch'iu. (Terra.)

CAPTAIN: Kuei-hsing? (What is your honorable name?)

OPARO: Pi-hsing Hsing-chün Yu-t'ai-chiao. (My humble name is Marching Jew.)

CAPTAIN: [Eyeing the "Wandering Jew" costume and makeup] Kuei-chia-tzu? (What is your honorable age?)

OPARO: San-chien i-pai-ling-i. (Three thousand one hundred and one.)

CAPTAIN: [Bursting out laughing] Hsin-hsi hsin-hsi! (Happy birthday!)

OPARO: Lao-chia. (Thank you.)

CAPTAIN: Pu-hsieh. Kung-kan? (You are welcome. What is your business here?)

OPARO: T'o-fu t'o-fu. Yen-p'ien ma-hsi-t'uan.

(Thank you for asking. We wish to put on our circus show for all of you.)

CAPTAIN: Ah? So. I jen nan ch'en po hito no aida. (By trying to please everybody one ends by pleasing no one.)

[But note his classy substitution of the cultured Japanese "hito no aida" for the final Chinese colloquial "jen i."]

At this point Winter broke into his lunatic version of the #2 Chief Rainier's fake Red Indian, delivered with dramatic passion.

"Whafoh you Chinky Chinamans alla samee chop chop? Ugh! No, no, no! Hit trail. Go aways. Vamoose back to rising sun. Ugh! Me takeum my circus show everywhere sun he shineum. Ugh! Nobody say vamoose. Everybody smokeum peace pipe. Ugh! Me payum all license cold cashly wampum. Me kowtow to all rules your great Manito hand down. Ugh! What you want, Chinky Chinamans? Wampum from Red Man? Me pay. Cashly. Got plenty in startepee. No talk with forked tongue." And here Winter thrust another pink gold slug into the astonished Captain's hand. "Smokeum peace pipe, yes? Ugh!"

The Captain of the main gate looked at Oparo. "What is that?" he asked.

"A foreigner from Terra," Oparo answered. (Wai-kuo-jeu ti-ch'iu.) "A red man." (Hung ti jen.)

"Does it have a name?"

"Chief Rain-in-the-Face." (Ta-yüan-shuai pei yü lun-che lien. Literally: "Generalissimo to-be-rained-upon face.")

The Captain couldn't help laughing. He knew it

was phony but it was wonderfully entertaining, and he now possessed one pound (Troy) of the rare Callisto pink gold, so the #2 Company of Chief Rainier's Indian Carnival was permitted to enter the Cathay Dome. It had become the Triton capital mostly because it had been built over the volcanic Meta mother lode. It was Winter's plan to search out the carefully guarded entrance to that lode. He had a volcano of his own in mind.

But he discovered, to his disgust, that the Captain of the main gate had had the last laugh. He had assigned the Hsing-hsing-ch'ang, the Cathay execution ground, as the location for the carnival. It was a square surrounded on three sides with some fifty arched brick gallows. On the fourth was a ramp leading up to the gibbet. The carnival was forced to set up surrounded by thirty corpses in various stages of grisly decay. A curious large iron box with what appeared to be a covered manhole on top stood in the center of the execution ground, serving no discernible purpose. Winter decided to use it as his huckster's podium.

And yet the grand opening of the carnival was turned into a gala by an execution. When the taped fanfares sounded but before Winter could mount the podium to exhort paying customers to "Hurry! Hurry! Hurry! Come one! Come all!" in Solaranto (*Hetzen! Hâter! Macht's schnell! Avanti unico! Bi istigh todos!*) the carnival filled with an excited mob of Jinks, men, women and children, all behaving as though they were anticipating a Mardi gras. But they looked every which way except at the sideshows.

There came a shrilling of birds. Winter looked up, expecting to see a flight of swifts or swallows (many of the Solar Domes contain birds, either by design or accident) but instead saw a flight of whistling arrows lofting overhead. The mob shouted, laughed, and did a sort of deadly tag game as the arrows fell. There were hoots when an unlucky received a razor slash. The execution grounds reeked of cruelty.

Then a thunder of gongs and rattle of wooden dragons announced the procession to the gallows; archers in black-lacquered antique armor and sallet helmets, musicians with their noisemakers, heralds bearing huge placards painted with crimson ideographs.

"Name, rank, and serial number of the executioner," Oparo whispered to Winter in Terran. "It's an honor every official gets, along with the Jink idea of a flourish."

"Doesn't sound like 'The Mikado' to me," Winter muttered, "or look it. Koko never made an entrance like this." He stared at the crimson-gowned executioner, borne on an open red palanquin, holding the free end of a noose garroted around a naked victim's neck. The man was dragged on all fours like a feral beast.

"Probably got busted for something big," Oparo said. "That's why they're hanging him."

"Christ! This is a bloodthirsty crowd."

"Wait 'till you see them at a Man-Shoot or a breaking on the wheel," Oparo grunted.

"I hope I never see it."

The procession went up the ramp, paraded

around the gibbet to a vacant arched gallows where the executioner knotted the free end of the noose overhead. He stepped back and nodded to the warriors, who notched arrows into their antique bows and began whistling shots at the victim's extremities, feet, knees, arms, while he danced and dodged, and the crowd howled into a final roar when the piercing agonies drove him off the edge of the gibbet into a last dance in space with his hands frantically clutching the rope while the archers shot them away. At last he shuddered and was still.

"Hai!" the mob exulted and turned to the lesser entertainments of the carnival. And yet, as the show went on hour after hour, they clued Winter in to the lead he was on the alert and hoping for. He noticed that the biggest spenders, the most carefree spenders, were men and women who all had one thing in common; each was missing a hand. He pointed that out to Oparo.

"Small-time goniffs," was the Mafia chief's judgment. "If you don't thief big, the Jinks settle for a hand. They chop the one you heist with. That'll be Big Money for the advice of the ages, turkey."

Winter nodded in amiable silence. He'd made his own unconscious judgments and entered the belly-dancer's tent where his teenyzapper was performing—not badly—for a score of lusty enthusiasts. He made lethal Maori sign to her. She flashed her eyes in answer, danced off the stage, and began enticing the paying customers one by one until Winter gave her the gig sign. When the performance was over, the audience left, not without coarse remarks to the turkey who was alluringly led into the teenyzapper's dressing room. Winter came out wearing the Jink's clothes, his face neutralized with the zapette's makeup. He hadn't bothered to discover whether she'd slugged the sucker unconscious or killed him. He really didn't care.

He paid his way into the snake-charmer's show, pleased that the box-office gorill didn't recognize him. He was even more pleased when Barb failed to recognize him when the performance was over and he remained in his seat. When she ordered him out, he knew he had passed the test and drifted out into the carnival but not on a random walk. "Pointer" was searching for his own *i-Shou*, which does not mean "pointer" in Jink; it translates as "one-hander." Winter was tightening up; his tactics were one long critical path.

He spotted a possible at last by the awkward way she received her change with her right hand from the hairy fire-eater. "Must be a natural lefty," he thought. "Let's see." It was difficult because she wore long, concealing sleeves. She was a squat woman, strong, beautifully dressed but without cosmetics, showing that she was unashamedly lower-class. (The Jink gentlewoman would rather die than appear in public without full makeup.)

Winter got his chance at last when she stopped at the Hindu magician's booth where the tired old hat bit was in progress. Out came rabbits and doves, and one bird fluttered directly at her. She threw up her hands automatically to protect herself, and the left was missing.

So he followed her when she left the carnival. His idea was that if she was a thief, connected with the Jink underworld, he could probably locate the Meta mine entrance through them. Their grapevine would be most likely to know, and he was prepared to buy the information with the irresistible pink gold.

You're wondering why he was operating solo and around Robin Hood's barn, so to speak. There were two reasons. The price he'd been required to pay for the cooperation of the Maori Mafia was the solemn pledge that he would do nothing to endanger their Meta connections on Triton. In fact, Oparo had refused to give him any information that might have been helpful. The second reason will be made manifest shortly.

He lost her in the streets and alleys crowded with hustling coolies, hawkers, merchants and gentry, and lined with ramshackle shops and hovels so rickety that they made him think of Sam'l Pepys' London and the Great Fire, when they tried to contain it with breaks by pulling houses down flat, merely using billhooks. She was going up an alley which could have been pulled flat, came to a crowded five-way intersection, and suddenly wasn't there.

Winter squirmed to the intersection and tried to look in five directions at the same time. They were warrens and she wasn't tall enough to be easily picked out in the crowds. *"Zolst ligen in drerd!"* he muttered bitterly, feeling the critical path tightening around his neck like a garrote. His wildly scanning eyes examined everything, searching for a clue, from a sophisticated tailor-shop where foreign style clothes were made *(hsi-fu-chuang)* to a group of coolies playing "Guess-Fingers" alongside a one-armed bandit.

The Jinks are notorious gamblers, all the way from guess-fingers through fan-tan, dice, cards, and roulette, to computerized Go. The authorities can't stop it, even if they wanted to, so they compromise by taking an enormous cut as a tax and the promotion of public gambling machines to compete with floating games. You can almost always get your percentage out of a locked coin box.

"Almost," because the Jinks are also notorious goniffs and can gaff any *apparat*. A host of slot machines kept being ripped off for payments without the correct percentage return; nothing in the coin box, not even counterfeit slugs. In desperation the Gambling Commission posted a "Thousand-Syce-No-Prosecution-Honest-To-God" reward if the ripper would step forward and tell all. The Rippees had to protect their cut. The perpetrator appeared, grinning, collected and revealed the scam. He was using ¼ Syce shoes cast in frozen CO_2 which evaporated within minutes.

Another corruption of their machines, unknown to the Commission, was synergized by Winter's unconscious phane sense. His reward was painful.

He couldn't stand still in the middle of the intersection; he didn't dare run the risk of attracting attention. He crossed to the one-armed bandit and started dropping ¼S coins and yanking while he thought hard. Keep on, chasing in all directions, hoping for a lead? Go back to the carnie and try all over again? Address these clowns shooting fingers at each other for Big Money in Solaranto, "Say, have you guys seen a one-handed woman lately?" Yeah. Sure.

He glared at the slot machine which displayed flower symbols instead of fruit; *shih-chu* (carnation), *pai-he* (lily), *ch'iang-wei* (rose), pansies, daisies, etc. He was in no mood to appreciate Jink aesthetics, but then he noticed that rosemary turned up on the right third dial at every turn and cancelled payoffs like the Vegas lemon.

"Machine's been gaffed," he muttered, dropping another ¼S and pulling the arm. Rosemary again. "Never give a sucker an even break. The Commission must be very happy with this number. All profit. *There's rosemary, that's for remembrance* . . .but where the devil's Ophellia *i-Shou?* To hell with it!" He dropped one more coin. Rosemary again. He took a last five-way con before returning to the carnival and, *mirabile visu,* spotted his Ophelia at the far end of the righthand alley, still talking to someone.

"We have ignition!" he exulted and shot down the alley. By the time he reached the intersection where he'd last seen his lead she was gone, but there was another slot machine there, this time without coolie accompaniment, but this time with the rosemary symbol showing on the left first dial. A strange tingling swam up into Winter's consciousness. He dropped a coin into the bandit and yanked. The dials spun free, but Rosemary for Remembrance again appeared on the left dial.

"By God!" he muttered. "By God!" He hung a left, peering past the buffeting crowds as he thwacked through, and there she was far ahead. The tingling had told him true.

He continued, no longer fretting when he lost sight of his *i-Shou*, but on the alert for one-armed bandits at strategic spots, and no longer dropping ¼S shoes. He knew he'd sensed the pattern; rosemary left, go left, rosemary center, straight ahead, rosemary right, turn right, and they would never change position no matter how often the machine was played, no matter what other symbols came up, and not more than one rosemary would ever show.

"It's the perfect gaff," he thought. "Like the old English 'Rogues and Vagabonds' road signs. I'd love to meet the genius who rigged this setup." He was signaled around another turn. "And what civilian could dig the scam? Not the casual Droppers. They'll shrug it off as bad luck and move on. Not the Commission. They won't question a big take. Not the fuzz. It wouldn't occur to them that a flower was saying, *Suivez-moi*. It's a miracle that I dug it."

As has been said, his seventh phane sense was an unconscious process.

The next time he caught sight of his *i-Shou* up ahead, she was entering a tottering pavilion. Three painted rosemary symbols were peeling over the door. "You are here," he thought, not feeling very brave, but he was committed.

"So much for Phase One," he told himself. He glanced at his chronometer. "Five hours to go. Now how do I prep for Phase Two? If this is some kind of gimpster sodality, it has to be strictly guarded, so there's no barging in offering bribes. No. Then what? Christjeeze! I'm playing this loose! What? What?" He thought in top gear and at last nodded. "Yes. Handle it like the mammoths. Don't try to fight their savvy. There have to be some brilliant minds among them to rig that bandit gaff. Make them fight mine, which is not so brilliant but an old hand at lying and misdirection . . ."

He cast around, searching for improvisation. The pavilion was on a lively lopsided square crowded with shops, stalls, offices.

Teahouse emitting music.

Undertaker offering "Boards of Old Age" and "Clothes of Old Age," the Jink euphemism for coffins and shrouds.

A Shrof, or money changer, the door curtained with strings of copper cash, Jink change even smaller than Big Money.

Apothecary.

Cutler, displaying knives and swords.

Fireworks.

Butcher, with a whole pig suspended over a charcoal roaster, broadcasting a delicious aroma.

"Paradise of Carnal Pleasure," also broadcasting a delicious aroma.

Shinto temple, decorated with wooden fish because fish, like the gods, never close their eyes.

So Winter improvised a riot, not by hiring the

carnal ladies to run naked through the square, as you might think. At the fireworks stall he bought a dozen Callisto rockets, not fussing about their colors. At the Shrof's he exchanged a half Syce for more strings of copper cash than he needed, not arguing about the traditional commission. He tied the strings to the rocket sticks while a small crowd of curious coolies gathered to watch. He fired the rockets in a barrage at the pavilion where they burst with spectacular displays and chiming showers of small change. He hurled the last strings at the roof. "Hai!" the coolies shouted and charged for the copper cash. Winter had his riot.

So did the pavilion. It was crawling up to the roof with grasping, searching, fighting scavengers, and spurting with jets of flame. A man came out, took one look and shouted an order to the interior. He was joined by a small task force of guards, and while they were trying to put the riot out, it was easy for Winter to slip inside unnoticed and unchecked.

If the pavilion was dilapidated outside, it was worse inside. He passed through a short labyrinth of unmanned checkpoints and found himself in a bare barn furnished with a few stools and benches. The walls were moldy and crawling with vermin, the ceiling peeling, the floor yawning with cracks. "Jigjeeze," he muttered. "I thought thieving paid. A mammoth wouldn't live here. Have I goofed following that *i-Shou* broad?"

Then his eyes accommodated and he noticed light shining up through the split floorboards. He searched, not too cautiously—the pandemonium outside would mask any noise he made—and located a flight of steps half-concealed behind a rotting tapestry crawling with lice. He winced but had to thrust the filthy cloth aside to get past. He descended softly on all fours, head foremost, until he was able to see the cellar. He was stunned.

There was a long tea chest in the center of the naked cellar. A coolie wearing blue denims was stretched out on the chest, left arm at his side, right arm stretched out with sleeve rolled up and hand over a white basin that seemed to be steaming. Two white coffers alongside the basin also seemed to be steaming. The coolie was writhing and restrained by four women and his *i-Shou* who were laughing and joking with him, and he was trying to joke back. It wasn't funny because a Jink surgeon with modern tools was amputating his hand.

The hand was an enormous laborer's paw and was clawed around something. And the hand glowed the dull red of embers, of hot iron, of a giant red star, of a dying nova—and suddenly the unbelievable pattern burst upon Winter. "My God! My God! My God! Like the Blacks who slashed their bodies to smuggle diamonds out of the African mines inside the wounds. These Jinks give up a hand to smuggle Meta out. The guards only check for the chill of cryogenic containers. Who'd believe anyone could be fool enough to smuggle barehanded?

"But they're no fools. A starving coolie can live forever in honor and luxury at the price of a hand which he could lose anyway in some other kind of rough labor. But this is only on a one-shot basis; large-scale commercial Meta smuggling must be using . . . what? Oparo called them small-time goniffs. He was right, but does he know what the big-time is? Yes, he must. Can I get it out of him?"

"Thank you so much, Rogue baby," a familiar voice called. Winter twisted around on his knees. Tomas Young, Terra's brilliant exobiologist who was also Triton's puissant Ta-mo Yung-kung, the Manchu duke, stood beaming at the head of the stairs with a small squad of grim soldiers behind him.

Chapter Eleven

THE TROJAN HORSE

In a duel, beware of the false attack. It is a deadly device, opening a path for the true lethal lunge.
> —Mousquetaire D'Artagnan

Yes, Tomas Young got away from us through an unheard-of piece of chicanery. He was an incredible polymath, versed in all the arts and sciences and using them to create brilliant tricks and devices, always keeping a step ahead of us.

For example, we knew that his prime ancillary action, outside of Intelligence, was the support, training and direction of the Solar Liberation Organization; and oh, the misdirection of titles! The SLO was dedicated to liberation. From what? Anything that angry failures blamed for their frustration; republicanism, capitalism, socialism, Marxism, you name it, tear it all down and stop the Solar from blocking our rightful climb to the top of the ladder.

Actually, the SLO was a gullible weapon in the class warfare waged by the feudal-minded Jink aristocracy determined on returning the Solar to the good old days of barons and serfs through the destruction of political and legal stability with the blunt instrument of terror. It was impossible to connect Young with this because his SLO recruitment and training was carried on in the mad-dog Domes of Titan.

We did succeed in penetrating the SLO just once and, with the hindsight which I detest, I realize that I should have anticipated the disaster. I sent one of our best and toughest agents—file name: "Terrier"—to the Brisbane Dome where he fought, savaged, and killed his way into attention and recruitment. Terrier could be ruthless when the mission required it.

One of the estimates of terrorist capability is what they call "The Black Room." The candidate is stripped bareass naked to prevent him from taking notes and sent into a pitch-dark room equipped with a flashlight. It's a simulation of an ordinary furnished living room and he's given five minutes to examine it and itemize everything in it.

When he comes out, his conscious memory is tested; how many chairs, pictures, tables, lamps, windows, etc. This is what he was told to remember. Then his unconscious memory is checked; were the chairs covered, what fabrics, were there playing cards on the table, what suits were showing, what scenes were depicted in the pictures, describe the lampshades, curtains, all the details he was not told to remember.

Terrier went in, spent his five minutes itemizing, came out and was instantly murdered. Damn Young! The Black Room was flooded with black light, and the absorption scars of the invisible *TerraGardai* I.D. tattoo on his skin showed unmistakably in the scanners. Damn me! I should have anticipated. I only learned the facts much later. Back then all I knew was that our best op had disappeared, *spurlos verschwinden*, and I was reduced to settling for surveillance of Young on Terra, and he came up with another conjuring trick.

We were monitoring his moves and he took that for granted. We took his "take" for granted. He took our "take" of his "take" for granted, and so *ad infinitum;* that's the business. Our basic was that if he made a move to leave Terra we'd stop him on some pretext or other. He didn't know that for sure, but he'd have done the same thing on Triton, so he was prepared for the possibility in New York.

I'd taken over a top-floor apartment across the road from the university Exobiology building and installed a *Garda* op, file name: "Granny Moses." She kept watch on his goings and comings and notified H.Q. by shortwave so that we didn't waste op time by having them hang around the building waiting for him to come out. Contrary to popular fiction, we handle more missions than one at a time. I conduct an orchestra in which everyone doubles and triples on instruments.

The Manchu was no fool, and his sensitive antenna warned him about Granny. Of course he didn't let on; he treated her the same way an amused neighbor would treat a nosy old woman who was always peeking out the window. He started by making faces at her, then smiling, then waving friendly-like. I'd instructed Granny to play it like a good-natured busybody, so she responded the same way. Eventually they were carrying on short conversations with gestures.

Then, this morning, the unheard-of happened.

Tomas appeared at the Exo building at his usual hour and Granny reported that he was in and would probably remain for a few hours, so his tail could take off, again as usual. But instead of remaining in the depths, playing exobio with his pet computer, the Manchu appeared in the window opposite Granny's on the tenth floor, and gave her a tragic wave. Granny waved back sadly too.

"It's a rotten world," he told her in sign language and she gestured back the same thing, wondering what the hell he was up to now. She found out. He opened the window, threw her a goodbye kiss, and jumped.

She saw him fall, hollered to H.Q. via shortwave, and tore downstairs to the street just as three other ops drove up like three screaming emergency squads. Granny Moses stared at the street. They stared at the street. Then they stared at each other. There was no body. There was nothing. A crowd had gathered, of course, and by the time they'd fought through and into the Exo-biology building, the Manchu was gone.

Yes, he'd done the unheard-of, long-range hypnosis. All that waving and smiling and gestured conversation back and forth had set Granny up for one moment of long-distance illusion. He'd slipped up to the roof and away on a silent chopper during the chaotic confusion down on the street. He was a dangerously resourceful adversary and, quite frankly, he outclassed me.

∘   ∘   ∘

Now back to the Manchu duke and Rogue
Winter in the Cathay Dome on Triton. What
followed that initial confrontation on the cellar
steps of the pavilion was appalling. Three armed
guards, not in ceremonial dress but in ominous
black, slipped past Tomas and Rogue and silently
gunned down every Jink in the cellar with their
handlasers. They dropped the severed hand with
its clutch of Meta nodules into one of the inert
helium coffers steaming alongside the long tea
chest, turned and waited for further orders.

Ta-mo Yung-kung nodded, motioned, seized
Winter's arm and took him up to the lopsided
square where another butchery had taken place.
The duke's black squad had lasered the pavilion
guards and coolies alike to make sure that no one
escaped. They were calmly plundering the bodies
while the pavilion roof still burned and spectators
craned from the safety of windows. The Manchu
duke smiled at the scene with satisfaction.

"You and your pathetic Trojan Horse," he
bantered as he led Winter, with a firm grip on his
elbow, through the crawling streets. The Manchu
was reenforced by three of his armed squad.
"Didn't you guess that I have sources in the
Turkish Domes? Better the Maori should have
trained their future king in spydom, or better still,
disguisery. That Turk jet painted into a totem
pole, and *you* painted into an Indian chief . . .
Pfui!"

Winter was silent.

"All the same I'm beholden to you, Rogue. You did lead me to the *Tsei-fei Tang* operation—That translates poetically as 'The Bandit Marching and Chowder Society.' Now I'll be able to break the Meta smuggling and I give you points for that. *Lao-chia!* We'll take a shortcut across the execution grounds. Did you catch our show this morning?"

"Yes."

"If I have any clout and—Don't even dream of signaling the carnival for help, baby—If I have any clout, and I do, you and the rest of your performing seals will get the same treatment. I'd hate to see an old friend condemned to *miao-chun t'ou.*"

"What?"

"Literally, 'An aiming at the head.' You barbarians call it a 'Man-Shoot.' " Young stopped alongside the iron box which Winter had been using as a huckster's podium, and tapped it. "We lock you in here with only your head showing. The archers take turns shooting until you're dead. Great entertainment." Young continued the progress, still gripping Winter's arm. "But I promise a last favor, lovey. If I can't swing a hanging for you and it's the box bit, I'll have a marksman drill a beam through your head as soon as the first arrow draws blood. I wouldn't want double-King R-og tortured for an hour. That would be *lèse majesté.*"

"Thanks."

"Of course the rest of your gang may be broken on the wheel along with the *i-Shou* gang, but I won't try to block that. The show must go on, how they say."

"Bread and circuses," Winter muttered.

"Skag and circuses on Triton," Young laughed and conducted his captive to a heavily guarded jade portal set in a high circular wall of beaten gold. "You are about to be honored with a visit to the Altar of Heaven, old friend, where you can make your peace with the Supreme Being." Young gave a crisp order and the portal was opened for them. "It's my red sash," he murmured. "Works wonders." He tapped his royal shoe.

Inside the golden wall were nine concentric terraces of white marble rising to a central tablet. "Imported from Carrara," Young commented as he led Winter up. "Each circle represents one of the nine heavens. Each is a multiple of nine slabs. Top circle, nine. Next lower, eighteen. Then twenty-seven, and so on down to the lowest heaven, which is the square of nine and the favorite number of our ziggy philosophers."

At the top of the exquisitely terraced mound was a central tablet. "This is *Shang-ti*, heaven, the center of the universe. Care to visit in the body, Rogue? Your soul will become a permanent guest sometime tomorrow."

They stepped onto the center of the universe together, and *Shang-ti* plummeted precipitously. It was so unexpected that Winter staggered and Young had to hold him upright. "You and your transparent Trojan Horse," he laughed. "Were you damned fool enough to imagine that any scam would lead you to this?"

"What *is* this?"

"Official entrance to the Meta lode."

"The hell you say!"

"The hell I don't."

"You mean for everyone? Workers? Guards? All trooping in and out through the Altar of Heaven?"

"No, no. V.I.P.s only. The *chien-ch'ang-ti,* the miners, are vetted in and out at the shaft heads which are concealed all over the Dome. No harm in telling you now, but you were within fifty feet of one when you staged that riot."

"I was? Where?"

"Inside the Paradise of Carnal Pleasures."

The center of the universe plunged past mysterious doors and hatchways and came to rest in an enormous ready room that echoed like a terminal. It was wheelshaped with the elevator shaft as its axis. There were a dozen heavy arched portals around the rim, each guarded by a sentry. They glanced at Young and snapped to attention.

"*Ch'ing-pien,*" he murmured. "At ease." To Winter, "The red-sash bit again. They revere it because it says the wearer is of the royal blood. Come on."

"Where?"

"You wanted to see our Meta mine, didn't you? So come on, already. I wouldn't want you to hang with unanswered questions on your mind, baby. That wouldn't be kind." And Ta-mo Yung-kung, Duke of Manchuria, thrust open a massive studded portal.

An exclamation was wrenched from Winter.

(The paradox of our time is that while we push out into the reaches of space we enclose our domestic lives into tighter moieties. Our spirit

yearns for man-made vastness but—ah, but, not a
gigantic exterior but a vast interior. What the soul
requires is the conquest of our own living space—
lebensraum—on a vast scale, which is why
enormous interiors overpower us.)

Despite the lethal pressures torturing him,
Winter's spirit was overpowered. He was in a
crystal cathedral of clouded glacial ice. The light
streaming through the open portal revealed a
vaulted Gothic ceiling hung with icicle-shaped
stalactites. It was supported by scores of ice
pillars soaring up from a black lava floor. A
motionless mist filled the frozen vastness. Then,
as Tomas closed the portal behind them, there was
pitch darkness which slowly brightened to a fiery
dusk produced by faint embers glowing inside the
pillars like tiny Christmas lights.

"Meta nodules," Tomas said, tapping a glow.
"Matter of fact, this is where Meta was discovered
two centuries ago. It was only a skinny tunnel
then. We knew about the lava ice tunnels of
course, twisty arteries fit only for rats and mice,
and we weren't much interested. At best they
could only be tourist attractions, and we never
want visitors on Triton."

"So I've heard."

"But a kid did some exploring in a termite
passage that only a kid could squirm through and
he saw a glow like one of these in the lava ice. He
broke through with his wooden clog, reached in
and pulled out a Meta nodule. He thought it was a
tiny jewel."

"So did I when I first saw them. Tiny opals."

"Naturally he ran home with his prize, not even wondering why his hand was starting to burn like hot iron. And that's how Meta was born."

"Was the kid rewarded?"

"How could he be? He died; just slow-burned to death. Anyway, even if we'd wanted to reward him, we wouldn't have known what for. It took our science types years to find out what that dumb kid's buried treasure really was."

"And so the dumb kid just did a slow burn."

"Once Meta starts its energy transformation, there's no stopping the nova."

"Short of amputation."

"You got it."

"Somehow I feel for the kid."

"That's the hang-up with you inner barbs; you all suffer from schmaltz."

"Unlike you chosen Celestials. Why don't you harvest these last numbers in here?"

"We need all the strength we can get to support the roof. The weight is tremendous . . . even with our low gravity . . . sometimes too much for the support limit. Then we get lava rock flows which swell up and block the passages, and a freak hazard we call 'shrapnel ice.' Fragments are exploded out of the pillars like bullets. We lose more damn coolies that way."

"Ah-so," Winter murmured and lapsed into another silence, but this one so pregnant that Tomas Young's hypersensitive antenna alerted. He swung Winter around and tried to search his face in the fiery glow.

"Wait a moment," he said slowly. "Am I

receiving your vibes, Rogue?"

"What vibes?"

"Another smuggling scam, perhaps?"

"Perhaps. If they can smuggle out a pound in a hand, how much inside a bod? All they'd have to do would be fake a shrapnel accident, rip a man open, pack him and haul the sad victim out with weeping and wailing."

"Murder?"

"You Jinks love killing for fun; why not killing for profit?"

"And that's how they get it out in quantity. Of course. The nova glow wouldn't show for hours. Not a clue to the guards that the corpse is packed with forty, fifty pounds of Meta. That has to be the pros. The one-hand bit? Strictly for loners who want to get rich. But systematic murder? Strictly professional. Who d'you think they pick for their patsies, Rogue?"

"Anyone they don't like. A loudmouth. A woman who's turned a guy down. Anyone who's too cozy with your fuzz. A faker. A phony. A freeloader . . ."

"Did your Mafia organize the scam?"

"Probably. I don't really know for sure. I may be the Maori king, but they don't tell me everything."

"All the same I give you points again, Rogue."

"Thanks."

"I wish we didn't have to kill you. I could use your synergy." The Manchu sighed. "Seen enough?"

"This can't be the whole mother lode."

"God, no! You can't see in the dark, but it goes on for miles. This is just the old worked-out section we use for display. Our visiting-dignitary show. The real thing is tunnels, stopes, beds and shafts crawling with coolies and cryo gear." Tomas sighed again. "So come on, baby, let's get your damn trial and execution over with. I won't even try to talk you into turning traitor and joining us. I know you're a born recusant."

Young had never relinquished his firm grip on Winter's elbow. Now he led him back to the portal and code-knocked. It was opened and they came into the blinding light of the ready room just in time to see the last of twenty large packing cases lugged in through another portal by a coolie gang. Each case was stenciled with a crimson crescent and star.

"Ah! A final treat," Young smiled. "Just in time to see a payment from our Turkish friends. Ahmet Tröyj is my most favored nation. His shipments are never late, never have to be weighed, and his raw skag and horse are always top quality. Care for a few bongs to anesthetize your upcoming unpleasantness, Rogue baby? We'll call it a mercy trip."

But as the coolies and guards ripped the cases open with happy anticipation, out of each sprang an armed Maori killer, and for a catastrophic minute the ready room echoed with the clash and screams of slaughter. Now it was Winter's turn to take a firm grip on the stunned Manchu's elbow.

"*This* is the Trojan Horse, Tom baby," he said pleasantly, steering the dazed man away from the butchering Slice Knives and the spreading blood. "I'd hoped for a rendezvous with our commandos, but wasn't sure I could zig it. I have to give you points for making it so easy."

Chincha, the massive commando chief, rolled up to Winter, blotched and smeared with blood. "We take the mine now?" he asked. "Oparo and the soldiers are waiting for the word from you."

"What? Take? Our mine?" Ta-mo gasped. "You're mad. All of you." He pulled himself out of shock. "You'd best surrender now, Rogue. I will be merciful."

Chincha applied the point of his Slice Knife to Young's throat unmercifully. "We are a hundred," he said, "and the match for any of your thousand. We take the mine."

"Never!"

"And then you do business with us on *our* terms."

"Never!"

The knife pricked a small gout of blood from Ta-mo Yung-kung's throat but it must be said that the Manchu never flinched. "You do business with us," Chincha repeated, "or we turn Triton into a baby sun with your Meta. King R-og has so ordered."

"Are you insane, Rogue?" Young shouted. "You've ordered a doomsday, a *Götterdämmerung* for all of us?"

"I ordered a hit," Winter answered, "and the Maori Maffia is prepared to go all the way. But we won't have to, Chincha," he added.

The commando chief gave Winter a hard, suspicious look.

"At least not this time," Winter grinned.

"Triton's top card has very kindly dealt himself into our hand. We've got the Manchu Duke of Death, and he outranks the King of the Mines and the Ace of Novas. He wins all pots for us. You get your Meta and I get my girl."

"You haven't got me, you damned fool!"

"No? Bring him along, chief. We'll exit via the V.I.P. route through the center of the universe and link up with Oparo."

"You'll never get me off Triton, Rogue."

"No? I'll trouble you for your royal sash, please. It's the passport out for me and my soldiers."

Young snorted. "Idiot! I'm Ta-mo Yung-kung. I'll be recognized with or without the sash."

"Will you, now?"

"One word from me at the main lock and your hundred will be broken on the wheel. Give up the heist, Rogue. You don't stand a chance. I promise to be merciful and I'll keep my word."

"Then we take the mine?" Chincha grunted.

"No, we take the duke."

Chapter Twelve

TRITON STANDOFF

When you meet your antagonist, do everything in a mild and agreeable manner. Let your courage be as keen, but at the same time as polished as your sword.

—Richard Brinsley Sheridan

Oh, they got the Duke of Death through the Cathay main lock and off Triton without any trouble to speak of; in fact the Manchu couldn't speak at all. In the first place he'd been stoned with GABA (gamma-aminobutyric acid from Barb's *Garda* service kit) which can make a Ganymede mammoth as manageable as putty. And in the second place we substituted him for the original Maori contortionist inside the Egyptian mummy wrappings. He could neither be seen nor heard, like a good little Duke of Death.

But not so angelic when they unwrapped him enjet to Ganymede; GABA wears off after four or five hours and the stifled passions return redoubled. Space is beautifully silent, but Young entertained the jet with the furious battery of his feet against the walls of his cubicle, rather like a percussion solo in a concert.

"We should of tooken his shoes off," Winter said.

"Better cool him before he starts banging his head," Barb advised. "You'll want him more or less *compos mentis* for the bargaining."

Winter nodded unhappily. He was faced with the most delicate and potentially explosive pattern he had ever tackled. How do you coax, charm, and/or threaten concessions from a formidable adversary who cannot be cowed by any known physical torture; an impregnable adversary who has commanded life and death for three quarters of a century?

"Talk about immovable objects," he muttered. "And I'm no irresistible force."

He knew what concessions he wanted from the Manchu; an ironclad Meta deal for his Maori Mafia—he'd promised that for Oparo's cooperation—and a safe delivery of his Titanian girl—he'd sworn that for himself. The problem was how to synergize these out of a hostage who only burned for a return to the celestial status quo and a frightful punishment for the Inner Barbarians.

"Use the Twelfth Commandment, baby, whatever the hell that may be," he murmured, undogged the hatch and stepped into the cubicle.

"Good morning, good morning, good morning, Mr. Young," he caroled. "Cheers, cheers, cheers, and welcome, welcome aboard. My name is Winter—Twinky Winter, they call me—your cruise director, and it's my happy job to make your excursion a happy trip on a happy ship. Now I've got you down to judge a beauty contest at lunch—ten lovely lovelies, and ties pay the judge, ha-ha—table tennis championship, a *thé dansant*, and—"

Young snarled.

"Feet hurt, Tom?"

Young snarled.

"Not funny, huh?"

"Nowhere."

"Well, you can't blame me for trying. The crew tells me you're unhappy."

"That's hardly the word."

"Figged off?"

"That's closer."

"Boiling mad?"

"At two thousand centigrade."

"Swearing eternal horrors for me and mine?"

"You got it."

"What's your version of horror, Tom? Trample us to death with your footsies?"

"Too much trouble."

"The noose?"

"Too quick."

"The wheel?"

"Not slow enough."

"The Man-Shoot?"

"Too final."

"I'm running out of horrors."

"Don't your Maori barbarians have any ideas of their own?"

"That's interesting, Tom. We've reverted to what you Celestials would consider simplistic. We don't believe in kills with frills. Kill-kwik is the name of our game. You saw that down in the mine. Slice-slice and bye-bye."

"Then what are you saving me for?"

"Who said anything about killing you?"

"Then why the snatch?"

"Do be sensible, Tom. We couldn't have zigged off Triton without you."

"What? Wrapped like a mummy? I'd laugh if I weren't drowning in gall."

"Yours or ours?"

"Both."

"Ah, but your gall gave us ours. Sympathetic magic, eh? And your sash gave me clout. By the way, here it is, returned with thanks. My teeny-zapper washed and ironed it for you. I think you may have inherited her from Ahmet Tröyj, Tom. Congratulations, but watch out for them scallops."

"Ha. Ha. Ha."

"Your gall laughing?"

"Look, Rogue, what the hell do you want?"

"As if you don't know."

"I want to hear it from you."

"Why, all we want is to be friends, Tom. The Mutual Marching and Chowder Society."

"Who's we?"

"Maori and Jink."

"What's your version of mutual?"

"That sacred word, revered in song and story . . . Togetherness. It's what makes the difference between marriage and divorce."

"Come on! Come on!"

"Straight talk, Tom?"

"When did you ever talk straight?"

"Then pragmatic?"

"Try."

"We want a Meta partnership."

"What!"

"I'm dealing for the Maori, and to hell with the Solar. Gouge the rest of the Solar as you please, but not us. We want a Meta partnership with you. We work with you, and you'll be in command, Tom. We get the Meta we want on an honest cost-plus basis, and your Jinks can keep the books. Straight, pragmatic business."

"Never."

"Just listen. How much of your market are we? Less than one percent. That's all you'll lose. And what do you get in return? Ten times that because we end the smuggling, and how much will that save you? I tell you, Tom, it's a damn good deal for both of us."

"Never."

"Jigjeeze, you inscrutables are a race apart. Why never? Twice?"

"Because you've shown me how to end the smuggling."

"Baby, baby, the Mafia can always come up with a new, improved scam."

"And your damned Mafia will rip us anyway."

"How?"

"We supply Meta at cost-plus and they bootleg it to the Solar at how much profit?"

"A point. A valid point well taken, but here's the answer. Instead of the Mafia joining you, *you* join the Mafia and you can all thief together happily ever after."

"You're crazy!"

"Why not? It'll be just another ancillary role for you. Odessa Partridge—who sends her profound awe—told me all about your Soho Young caper and the decoy agent ring you were running. So now you can run the Mafia ring and pocket your cut."

"And I'm supposed to believe you're giving yours away?"

"Giving what away? I'm the Maori double-kill king, and even that's too much for me. I certainly don't want any part of the bootleg bit. It can be all yours."

"It can be all mine without any help from you."

"Not while you're my guest."

"Release is part of the deal?"

"Natürlich."

"What else?"

"My girl back."

"Your girl?"

"My Titianian. You offered to examine her pregnancy. Remember?"

"We haven't got her."

"I know that, but I've got a syntuition that your agents know where she is and can't get at her. Fact? Level with me, Tom. There's a hell of a lot at stake."

"What good will it do you?"

"If I know where she is I'll be able to get her back. You know where she's holed up? Fact?"

"Yes. Fact, and that's *my* winning card."

"Maybe. Maybe. Business first."

"No."

"No what? Meta? Release? Girl?"

"No cooperation with you in any sense, in any ever, and now what card will you play? Death?"

"Out of the question, Tom. I need you as much

as you need me."

"Torture?"

"A possibility."

"Did Odessa Partridge also tell you how the Ganymede Zulus snared me when I was under another cover and gave me the jungle grill trying to roast information out of me? They couldn't."

"I believe you."

"The torture hasn't been invented that can break me, and I've gone through some savage ones."

"You *are* a challenge."

"You'll get nothing from me except what I want."

"What do you want, Tom? What's your price?"

"You have fireplaces in your Dome?"

"Are you bargaining or chatting?"

"Do you?"

"Only the royal palace and the tribal chiefs; Oparo, Chincha, and so forth. Status symbol, that's all."

"With polar bear rugs on the hearth? Whole head and white hide?"

"Mammoth. Not very attractive."

"I've got a Delft tile fireplace. I want your head and hide for the hearth rug, and I want your head taken off your living skinned body last of all. Slow!"

"With me screaming in B-flat minor? I have the funny feeling that you're not fond of me, Tom."

"Or better still—What did that *Garda* woman shoot me with?"

"A GABA derivative. Intelligence uses it to make

rattlesnakes amiable enough to wait on table."

"Better still, I'm going to slug you with this GABA and use your living bod for a hearth rug."

"Be practical, Tom. I couldn't just lie there under your hooves forever. I'd have to be fed and taken to the bathroom now and then."

"No way. When you piss and shit, your Maori pigs will lick it clean, and you'll eat their raw flesh."

"Gee! That's awful, Tom. I'll be living on capital. Do me one favor, feed me the teenylaundress first; I've already tasted her tushy. You'd remember her—the sexy belly-dancer—if you weren't such a fuckin' faggot."

"Zag it, Rogue!"

"Oh, it's no secret, baby. I've always known. You're my favorite closet queen, but alas, alas, cruelty, thy name is faggot. Apologies to W. Shakespeare. D'you think Hamlet was gay? That sick mamma hangup . . . "

"By God, I'll—"

"And now that computers are half-organic—that tank of yours on Terra, the trick you're having the love-hate affair with—it sucks, doesn't it?"

"Christ damn you!"

"I see it does. Fascinating, isn't it? Now that we can connect with our quasi-human computers—I swear my workshop tank is more alive than I am—we can have love affairs with them. We can even have togetherness by radio, telephone and telegraph. Does your trick go down on you by shortwave when you're on Triton?"

"I swear you'll be forever dying."

"Will I aunty? Thank you for cluing me in to your torture." Abruptly, Winter turned into cold iron. "Last time around the track, Manchu. Is it a Meta deal?"

"Never."

"Do I get my girl's location?"

"Never."

"How long did the Zulus roast you?"

"A week."

"And you didn't break?"

"Never."

"I'll break you in a week, Manchu, and I'll do it no-hands."

Chapter Thirteen

BALLADE DE PENDU

In which the humiliation of a formidable
adversary leads to a search of two lovers for
each other through the grapevine of the
secret gossip and tittle-tattle of the
Worshipful Company of Computers.

—The author

THE NEW YORK ZOO

presents

THE CARNIVAL OF CREATURES

featuring

Gorilla, the Good
Bear, the Bewildered
Wolf, the Worried
Lemur, the Lost
Orang, the Outcast
Seal, the Sport
Elephant, the Ecdysiast
Hyena, the Hypocrite
Otter, the Oppbrecher
Mammoth, the Moocher
Chicken, the Chicken
and

s t a r r i n g

RINGMASTER, THE FIEND IN HUMAN SHAPE

production directed by

Nigelle Englund

(The Producers and Theatre Management
are Members of the Solar League of
Eco Theatres and Producers, Inc.)

Admission Free

(Adults must be accompanied by Children)

FIRE NOTICE: *Thoughtless persons annoy patrons and
endanger the safety of others by lighting a stash,
bong, or water pipe for a quick hit in prohibited
areas during the performances and intermissions.
This violates a City ordinance and is punishable by
law.*

This dirty, rotten ringmaster (HISS!) armed with a red-hot whip (BOO!) was torturing the sweet, harmless animals (OOH! AHH!) into leaping through flaming hoops, juggling burning bricks, and riding electrical velocipedes which shocked them with lightning bolts. (BOO! HISS! GRRR!) Then a determined ape rebelled. (CHEERS!) The other animals joined him. (*"Creatures of the world unite! You have nothing to lose but your chains!"*) (HOORAY!) The vicious ringmaster was overpowered, (LAUGHTER! JEERS!) and forced to perform the same humiliating antics with his own whip. (APPLAUSE! ECSTASIES!)

After the curtain fell, the stagehands rearranged the sets, props, and life-size animal marionettes for the next performance. Only the ringmaster puppet was walked off the stage on its wires into a dressing room in the wings where Nigelle Englund, the albino vet. and zoo director, and Rogue Winter were waiting.

While Nigelle detached the wires and removed the acupuncture needles from hypnogenic control spots in the puppet's body, Winter said, "Nice show this morning, Tom. Better than last night. Much better. You're really getting into the part. I clocked forty laughs and ten boffs."

Ta-mo Yung-kung, Number-One Jink Mandarin and Manchu Duke of Life and Death, snarled helplessly.

"You're great in the role, Tom. The kids love to hate you. Nig says you're the best attraction the zoo's had in years."

"If . . . I . . . Could . . . Only . . . "

"Now, now! No actor's temperament, Tom. No fooling around with your part. You're acupunctured for a taped performance and you'll have to stick with the script. The show's the boss."

"We can't keep this up forever, Rogue," Nigelle said. "Even with rest periods between shows, he's bound to run out of vital juices and turn into a vegetable."

"All I need is a week to smash his *amour propre*, Nig. No faggot's vanity can hold out longer than that."

**and
starring
RINGMASTER, THE FIEND IN SNARLING SHAPE**

"Tom, you were really brilliant tonight. When Gorilla, the Good shoved that hot brick up your ass, your pain-take brought the house down."

Ta-mo Yung-kung, Number-One Jink Mandarin and Manchu Duke of Life and Death, glared help-lessly.

"Yeah, I know, they're rewriting the script. But you have to understand, Tom. Great scripts aren't written, they're *re*written. That's show business."

and
starring
RINGMASTER, THE FIEND IN GNASHING SHAPE

"I don't know whether that sight-bit of Seal, the Sport flipping sardines into your mouth after you jump through the hoops really works, Tom. And I'm definitely against the Ecdysiast dumping excrement on you like that. Bad taste. Very bad. It should go, even if the kids love it.

"But not to worry, baby. Nig Englund's scheduled a script conference for tomorrow and we'll work something out. May even call in a couple of gag writers from the Coast. Got any suggestions? People you'd like to work with?"

Ta-mo Yung-kung, Mandarin and Manchu Duke, groaned helplessly.

and
starring
RINGMASTER, THE FIEND IN WHINING SHAPE

"Hot news, Tom! Headlines! You've become a cult figure. The kids are starting Ringy-Ding clubs all over the Solar. They wear your photo—the great shot of Gorilla, the Good shoving the brick up your ass—and they carry red whips. They call their bluejeans 'bluefiends.' Best of all, a lot of grown-ups are recognizing your picture and are

coming here to find out why the famous exobiologist is making a clown of himself. Your Jink
chums are coming, too. Triton can't believe that
their Celestial mandarin is playing the *meshugena
zhlob* in a zoo show, and they've got to see for
themselves. You're a star, baby. We'll have to program you for signing autographs.''

Ta-mo Yung-kung, Mandarin and Duke, sobbed
helplessly.

and
starring
RINGMASTER, THE FIEND IN SHOWBIZ SHAPE

"And now, ladies and gentlemen, persons,
people and hybrids HA-HA everywhere, alive and
kicking HA-HA from the New York zoo to every
nook and granny GET IT? of the Solar, SBC-TV
brings you the latest, the greatest, the cutest, the
brutest clown in variety history in the preem of
his brand-new, grand new, vulgar, venomous,
vengeful hate-filled variety miniseries, starring
the man you love to hate—THE RINGMASTER in
—THE RINGY-DING DUNG SHOW!''

"Five minutes, Mr. Young. Onstage, please.''

"Gig, Tom baby. We've got you wired and programmed to wow them. You're going to make
yourself and Triton so famous you'll become
catchwords. And I can say I knew you when you
were nothing but a Duke of Death. So . . . Let's go.
Good luck. *Merde.* Break a leg . . . ''

"Com . . . Pute . . . Err . . . '' the Manchu
croaked.

"What, baby?''

"Com . . . Pute . . . Err . . . Know . . . "

"A computer knows?"

"Y . . . "

"A computer knows what? Hurry up, Tom. You're on in three minutes."

"Wheh . . . Yuh . . . Girl . . . "

"Where my girl? Where my girl is? A computer knows where my Titanian is holed up? Where your soldiers can't get at her?"

"Y . . . "

"What computer? Where?"

" . . . "

"Come on, Tom. Don't play games with me. There are millions of tanks in the Solar. What particular computer knows where my Demi is?"

" . . . "

"Come on, damn you! You're broke. Don't try to weasel. Deliver. What computer and where?"

" . . . "

"It's no use, Rogue," Nigelle said. "He can't. He's completely drained . . . pure puppet now. God knows how long it'll take him to recover his conscious self.'

"Yeh. Might as well wire him up for his show. I've got to compliment the sonofabitch; he held out for six days. I also have to compliment myself; I broke him no-hands . . . but I'm left nowhere, owing to a surfeit of hay."

"What?"

"Needle in the haystack, Nig. First find that goddam computer, which could be any tank anywhere, and if it'll tell me the truth."

"Computers can't lie."

"They're half-alive, aren't they? Name any living

thing that doesn't lie, one way or another."

"If so programmed."

"And who's to say this Manchu turkey hasn't so programmed the tank that knows where Demi's stashed herself? You know, tell the truth only and if the password code is keyed in to you."

"It *is* tricky."

"And so is finding her even if a tank can tell me where to look."

"How do you figure that?"

"Common sense, Nig. If our Duke of Death could tell his soldiers where to find her, and they still couldn't grab her, she must be absolutely inaccessible. *Oi veh, meyd'l! Tsibeles* is growing in my *estomac!*"

o   o   o

I have this absurd fantasy of Rogue and Demi walking the streets of New York looking for each other. Chances are a jillion-to-one against their meeting because when he's searching downtown she's headed up, and when she turns east, he turns west.

But in this silly drama of mine they happen to approach the same corner from opposite sides of a crossroad and are, against all odds, bound to meet. Only at that moment a giant theater billboard is lowered to the sidewalk at the corner so that the electric bulbs can be changed. Rogue passes around the outside of the sign and Demi slips past on the inside, and they never meet. The billboard is advertising, FATE—NOW PLAYING AT THE BIJOU.

And yet this little farce is inspired by the reality which both later confided in me; they were searching for each other through the grapevine of the Honorable Company of Computers which is far more labyrinthine than the streets of a city.

In a most unexpected way computer technology has reversed prosthesis, which is the addition of an artificial part to replace a defect in the body. The engineers discovered that the addition of organic parts to a computer enlarged it from a mere lightning adding machine into a quasi-living entity. But a side effect no one could have anticipated was the transformation of the tanks into a grapevine of crosstalk.

Demi Jeroux was working inside the grapevine in her search for Winter. See how their semilife peeps through the computer gibberish:

```
!PRINT "ALL POINTS BULLETIN = APB"
APB
!PRINT "ROGUE WINTER = ROG"
ROG
!PRINT "R-OG UINTA = ROGUE WINTER =
ROG"
ROG
!PRINT "TERRA = T"
T
!PRINT "GANYMEDE = G"
G
!PRINT "TRITON = TT"
TT
READY
!
APB ROG TGTT
T
?T
?
```

```
900        REM***SEARCH GENERATOR***
1000       CLS
1010       INPUT "COMPUTERS (C)" ; A$
1020       INPUT "ANALOG & DIGITAL (A,D)" ; #
1030       CLS : IF A$ = "A" OR A$ = "D" THEN # =
           INFORM
1040       IF # = "A" INFORM
1050       IF # = "D" INFORM
1060       PRINT APB LOCATION ROG
                         NO SIGNIFIES 'NUMBER'
                         0 SIGNIFIES 'ZERO'
                         0 IS A NUMBER
                         NO = R-OG UINTA
                         NO = ROGUE WINTER
                         O = NO R-OG UINTA
                         O = NO ROGUE WINTER

1070       THANKS LOADS A HEAP & YOU ARE N =
           NERD

!!         REM***MAIN PROGRAM - ROG CAPTURE***
10         GOSUB 1000 ROGUE WINTER
20         GOSUB 2000 R-OG UINTA
30         ROG = "RANDOM = R"
40         ROG APB = R"
50         GOSUB TERRA "T" ; GOSUB GANYMEDE "G"
60         IF ROG = "T" THEN APB "T"
70         GOSUB APB ROG TGTT JUST IN CASE
80         IF NO = 0 & 0 = NO ROGUE WINTER THEN
           WHERE?

                         LOOKING FOR YOU STUPID
                         AND YOU CAN STICK 1070
```

On the other hand, Winter was working outside the party line, trying to tap it for clues to Demi's hideout, and not at all aware that it was a grapevine which kept its own secrets. He cross-examined scores of computer tanks, speaking compiler, assembly, and machine languages, and here are examples of some of the answers he received:

00101101110001011001010110000111

and

 ᛁ   ᛁᛁᛁ   ᛁ   ᛁᛁ ᛁᛁᛁ   ᛁ   ᛁᛁᛁ   ᛁ
 ̲   ̲   ̲̲   ̲   ̲ ̲   ̲̲   ̲

and

:.::..:..:...::..:.....::..::...:

That last reply translates as, "A random variable on a sample space with its admissible system of events and probabilities measure is a function with the property that for every real number there is an event in the admissible system of events."

"Thanks loads a heap," he growled.

"A field is a commutative division ring," the tank added helpfully.

Perhaps most exasperating was the fact that he, a professional mavin of languages, had been forced to go through a primer to accustom him to the niggling linguistics which all tanks demand. It was a sort of White Knight's dialogue with Alice in "Through the Looking-Glass."

The name of your search is called *"Needle in the Haystack."*

Right. That's my search.

Wrong. That's what the name is *called*. The name really is *"Come out, come out, wherever you are."*

Right. That's what my search is called.

Wrong. Your search is called *"Quiz the Computers,"* but that's only what it's *called.*

Then what the hell *is* my search for my girl?

Ah, now we're getting there. Your search really is *"APB Demi Jeroux."* Now pay attention. Computers demand four linguistic identities; the call-name of the name of the search, the name of the search, the call-name of the search, and the search. Got that?

C'est la mer à boire.

What?

It's going to be impossible. Like swallowing an ocean.

o   o   o

Now that you know all about my inaccessible hideout, Odessa, you can understand how I knew everything Rogue said and did when he returned to his *Beaux Arts* apartment, angry and exhausted.

I was eavesdropping, true, but a girl in love has got her rights. Who said, "All's fair in love and war"? Some poet named Francis, I think. Not Francis Scott Key, Francis Smedley who ran the "Stars and Bars Soda Solarium (No Singles)" just outside the Marymount dormitories.

Rogue'd repossessed my psycat (whose name was "Coco") from Nig Englund and was pouring out his frustrations to her. Coco, of course, was

clinging to his neck, making churrs of
contentment. I admit that I was a bit envious
because I wanted to do the same thing myself, but
Rogue had to be carefully prepared for the
surprise; the Maori macho pride, especially that of
a double-kill king, can quick-fire.

Anyway, he was complaining, "Damn it,
madame, I tried the Triton tank in their embassy.
Now that I've got their prize mandarin, they
couldn't have been more cooperative. Then the
Solar Media number. Missing persons. Her apart-
ment house. Anywhere she had a charge account.
Then Alitalia, United, TransSolar, Jet France,
PanSol. Long distance to Virginia. Odessa
Partridge and her Intelligence *apparat*. Tom
Young's exobiology trick. I tried *Elektronenrech-
ners, Ordinateurs, Calcolatores, Comhairims*, and
even the old, original Golem-One computer in
Jerusalem. Nothing nowhere. Null. *Nada. Nulla.*
I'm licked!"

He loosened the collar of his jumpsuit and
opened it to give my psycat access to his throat.
Then he toured the apartment fretfully, inspecting
every piece of furniture I'd used, every picture
and book I'd examined, the knickknacks and
souvenirs which I'd touched; the six-foot tub
which we'd never had the chance to use together;
the Japanesey bed which we had. Then he went
into his workshop to switch on the computer to
which he was neurally synapsed. It was already
on.

"Crazy," he muttered. "I must have been walking in my sleep . . . unless you did it, kitkat?"

"Spqrrr," and that was no answer.

He did activate the tank's auxiliary video screens located around the apartment so that he could wander while debating with his second self and see what answers it displayed. He was flabbergasted to see the screens displaying both of us seated on the living-room couch, talking to each other that first night.

"But the computer wasn't switched on that first night. I could swear to that."

ROGUE

What did you like about me?

DEMI

When?

ROGUE

When you first came to work for *Solar Media.*

DEMI

What makes you think I liked you?

ROGUE

You were willing to have lunch with me.

DEMI

It was your mad passion.

ROGUE

For what, in particular?

DEMI

The sophisticated beauty in the ski lodge, Mystique d'Charisma.

ROGUE

There isn't any Mystique d'Charisma.

DEMI

That's what I liked about you.

"But the talk wasn't like that at all, our first night together. This is all ass-backwards!"

DEMI

Would you like an autographed skin shot of Mystique? I can get the *Media* art department to fake it for you.

ROGUE

No thanks. I want more than faked nudes from you.

DEMI

He's turning macho. Now that he's made the girl, he's showing his true colors.

"What the hell is going on with this damned demented tank? The voices and figures are perfect, but the dialogue is a distortion."

DEMI

And what did you like about me when you first met me at *Solar?*

ROGUE

Who says I liked you?

DEMI

You moved in on me like a bandit and asked me out to lunch . . . and maybe worse.

ROGUE

It was your gaydom.

DEMI

You thought I was a fag in drag?

ROGUE

No, no, your gayety. You do everything like it's
fun and games, and you're completely unex-
pectable. You—You're a gay deceiver.

DEMI

Meaning I'm a liar.

ROGUE

Meaning you're a sprite.

DEMI

Yes, they all call me "Tinkerbell."

ROGUE

And I do believe in fairies.

DEMI

If you believe in fairies, clap your hands.

*"I dig! I dig! The tank is telling it from her point
of view; how she'd like to remember it or how she
wishes it'd happened. She must have recorded this
bijou for me when she came up here to leave her
cat and key before zigging off on the lam."*

ROGUE

This is a damned lymphatic start for anything.

DEMI

Why? Isn't it full of fun and games? That's what
you said you liked about me.

ROGUE

Who's having fun?

DEMI

Me.

ROGUE

Who's playing games?

DEMI

Your gay deceiver.

ROGUE

So where do I come in?

DEMI

Just play it by ear.

ROGUE

The left or the right?

DEMI

The middle ear. That's where your soul dwells.

ROGUE

You're the damnedest girl I ever met.

DEMI

I've been berated by better men than you, sir.

ROGUE

Like who?

DEMI

Like the ones to whom I refuse the worst.

ROGUE

You leave me in doubt.

DEMI

Yes, that's the only way to handle you.

ROGUE

Damn it! I'm outclassed.

"Surprise! Surprise! This reenactment is pretty close to what really happened. Evidently Demi rather liked it. Wonder what made it so special for her."

DEMI

This is the last thing I expected from you.

ROGUE

What last thing?

DEMI

Your being shy.

ROGUE

Me? Shy!

DEMI

Yes, and I like it. Your eyes are taking inventory, but the rest of you hasn't made a move.

ROGUE

I deny that.

DEMI

Do you know John Donne's love poems?

ROGUE

I'm afraid not. Must have busted them, owing to a surfeit of something.

DEMI

All Virginia girls read them and sigh. I'm going to act one out for you.

ROGUE

I am not afraid.

DEMI

"Licence my roaving hands, and let them go,
Before, behind, between, above, below."

ROGUE

Now I am afraid.

DEMI

"O my America! my new-found-land,
My kingdome, safeliest when with one maid
   mann'd . . .
How blest am I in this discovering thee!"

ROGUE

Demi, don't. Please don't.

DEMI

''Full nakedness! All joyes are due to thee,
As souls unbodied, bodies uncloth'd must be,
To taste whole joyes.''

ROGUE

I beg you . . .

DEMI

''To teach thee, I am naked first; tonight
Why needst thou have more covering than
    thy sprite?''

ROGUE

Demi!

DEMI

Come on, Rogue . . .

*''Jigjeeze! Did she tape her version of us together
in bed that night?''*
Oh, I did, I did. In the darkness he seemed to be
a hundred men with hundreds of hands, mouths,
and loins. He was a Black with a thick tongue that
choked me, and hard, high strokes that shuddered
deep into me.

He was a succulent, crooning in my ear while
his mouths drank arpeggios from my skin, before,
behind, between, above, below. He was an
outworld animal emitting guttural grunts as he
bestialized me and wrenched ecstatic moans from
my belly. He was tough, tender, demanding,
savage, macho, macho, macho. My loins trembled
in an earthquake of endless spasms.

And yet through all this we were carrying on a
sparkling conversation over champagne and
caviar as an erotic prelude to lounging before the
fire to share love for the first time, and after the
first kiss he placed a ring on the third finger of my
left hand, a pink-gold seal ring engraved with a
Virginia flower.

Winter was jolted to his feet.

"Go to black!" he shouted to his half-self.

The screens faded.

He took a deep breath. He could have thought
the command, but now he knew that the computer
was in business for itself, and he suspected why.
"She couldn't know about the ring," he said
slowly. "She'd already split from the Triton
soldiers when I was buying it. She never saw it.
She never heard about it. Unless . . . Unless . . ."
He paced. "It was a greater synergist than I who
said, 'Elementary, my dear Watson.' And so it is.
And I'm a complete idiot. No wonder the Jink
gorills couldn't get at her." He raised his voice.
"Program Problem APB Demi Jeroux Print
Absolute Address." Then he sat down and waited.

He didn't know what he was expecting; a street
or CB number, perhaps, or the image of a house,
office, terminal, a city, a continent, a satellite, a
planet, a river, a lake, an ocean. *His* tank knew
where Demi was. He knew that an "absolute
address" in computer circles demanded the exact
storage location where the referenced operand is
to be found, and no weaseling before, behind, between, above, below and out of the imperative.
Certainly he never anticipated this as the screens
brightened:

"#$%__&')(*+:=-;#."

"What the hell is that?"

"*#)$(%'__&+."

"Are you trying to tell me something?"

"#*$*%*__*&*'*()*)(."

"Oi veh! Me Good Indian; who you?"

"+=:;*-o)o(#&=+."

"Would you mind telling me what language you're speaking . . . if language is the word?"

",.;=o-*+:?#)(."

"Care to try another? Solaranto, maybe, or even TankSpek? You know, one plus one equals whatever you're programmed for."

"-"

"Is that a 'no'?"

"+"

"Is that a 'yes'?"

"+"

"Ah, now we're getting somewhere. Let's play Twenty Questions. Are you animal?"

"+"

"Vegetable? Just to make sure of your + and -."

"+"

"Both? You throwing curves? Mineral?"

"+"

"All three? Now what could possibly be all three; animal, vegetable, and mineral? Man? Maybe, if you count prosthesis, and a lot of us are prosthetic these days. Machine? Maybe. Food? Maybe. Some seasonings are mineral. But Man doesn't speak your kind of language. Neither do machines. That leaves Food. Ah, food! It speaks a lovely language of taste and smell and—"

Winter was jolted again.

After a chaotic moment he burst out, "Dear
God! Dear trustworthy, loyal, helpful, friendly,
courteous, kind God, I thank Thee, and someday
I'll do *You* a good turn. Of course! Elementary, my
dear Watson. Scents, tastes and sensations—the
Titanian chemical language. That's what the tank
is trying to translate into visual, simply because
it's not equipped to project taste and touch. No
computer is. Maybe they should be someday. All
the same, I'm impressed, really impressed; I didn't
think we had it in us. So gig, go ahead with the
program. Tell me all in Titanian. Where the hell's
Demi Jeroux?"

*

"Yes?"

**

"Yes?"

**
*   *

"Go ahead."

**
*   *
*   *

"Keep on talking."

"A halfmoon, maybe? Sort of standing on its ear?"

"A circle. Yes. And?"

"The circle's divided into two. And now?"

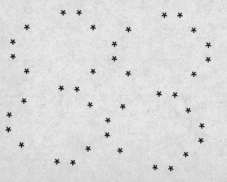

"And now four? Wait a minute. Wait. Just. One. God. Damned. Minute. This pattern rings a bell. Bell. Bell. Bell. Bellboy. Bellpull. Belladonna. Bell jar. That's it! The bell jars covering the instruments in biology lab at Tech. Biology. Cell cleavage into blastulation. Then the gastrula. Embryology, that's what I'm seeing. Something's being born. What? Where? What the hell kind of message is this?"

He was hypnotized by the display of lightning cell division; blastula, gastrula, blastodisc . . .

"My God! It's going in microseconds."

Ectoderm, mesoderm, endoderm . . .

"This is the first time in history that a computer's ever given birth, but to what?"

Primitive Streak . . .

His excitement drove him into the workshop to get a better view of the end product on the giant prime video of his computer. During those few moments the development had accelerated into its *dénouement*, for he arrived just in time to have the huge screen explode into his face. Demi Jeroux burst out of the computer in a shower of plastic particles, rolled and sprawled on top of him. She was naked, sweating, trembling.

"Golly!" she gasped. "Getting in was easy compared to getting out. Are you hurt, darling?"

"I'm fine. I'm great. I'm ennobled. I'm stupefied. Hi, hey. Hi, my love. Hi, my darling sprite. What's a nice girl like you doing in a place like that?"

"Surprised?"

"Hell no. I always knew we had it in us. I knew it all along."

Chapter Fourteen

Terra Iincognita

Ah, me! What a world this was to live in two or three centuries ago when it was getting itself discovered! Then Man was courting Nature, now he has married her. Every mystery is dissipated. The Solar is as familiar as the trodden pathway running between towns. And if you believe that, you're *meshuge*.

—Odessa Partridge

This time they left the six-foot tub together and dripped into the living room. They sat on the couch with their feet up on the coffee table, saturating everything with bath water and not giving a damn in their joy over the final resolution of their crises.

"You ought to hear the furniture and rugs complaining," Winter laughed. "Glug, glug, glug. Glgglglg. Glooog, glooog, glooog. There's no pleasing some things."

"I'm a pleased thing," Demi glowed. She was looking like a Nereid reclining on a wave; red flowing hair, green eyes, coral-pink skin. "I never dreamed sharing love under water could be so—so—"

"So what?"

"I can't say. Nice Virginia girls never talk about it, so I have no words. Did *you*, ever before?"

"Many times," Winter answered promptly. "I've been a rogue under all kinds seas; sea salt, season's greetings, sea lions, a seesaw, a bishop's see, the Zuider Zee dam—" She shut him up with a smack.

"And while I was gone?"

"What, while you were gone?"

"You know what. Was there anyone else? I promise I'll understand," and she began to look like Whistler's mother.

"Get out of the rocking chair," he grinned. Then, seriously, "Believe me, love. We all chase; not because we're lecherous, we're simply looking for variety and novelty, for entertainment. Well, every time with you it's new and different, so I don't have to chase anymore. The answer is no. I was happy to wait for my entertainment. Also, I was too busy trying to locate my variety show and get her back."

"You're my favorite Starshmykler," she beamed, transforming into her idea of a blushing *meyd'l*. "Now I want to hear all your adventures that weren't reported by the computer grapevine."

"No, you first."

"But I haven't had any. How could I, cooped up in your rotten old tank?"

He hesitated. "Well, which do you want, the good or the bad?"

"The bad first. Let's get that over with."

He nodded somberly. "You couldn't know this," he began slowly, "but on Triton I got trapped in one of their deadly ice lava caves for hours and hours. No food, no water, no light. The only thing that kept me going was thinking about you and dreaming of all the wonderful exciting new patterns we'd play together when and if I could ever find you."

"But you did escape, Rogue. Obviously. How?"

"Finally, in desperation, I reverted to the Maori

savage and clawed at the ice and lava with my bare hands like a trapped animal, and at last I opened a hole just big enough for me to squeeze through to the outside, but . . . ''

"But what?"

"But when I got out I saw my shadow, so I went back in."

She let out a little shriek. "Oh, you, you, you! You had me believing! Liar! Wicked Rogue liar! You'll tell lies in your coffin."

"Yeah, to the pallbearers. So how did you get into the computer? It only opens up to me and no one else. Showed it your shadow?"

"Well, after I broke away from the Jink hitmen—"

"How?"

"Mace."

"I didn't know you had any."

"I don't, but I kept screaming 'Mace' at them in Titanian chemical and it finally had the same effect."

"My God, love, you're something to cope with."

"Indeed yes. I'll never have to 'have a headache' with you, I can always cool you with chemical, not that it's very likely with my one and only Starstud. Anyway, I came up here with the cat, let myself in with the key, and did some hard thinking. Was there any hiding place where I could survive and the Jinks couldn't get at me again? The only one I could think of was your tank, so I went in."

"But it only opens up to me."

"You left it on."

"Maybe I did, but it still won't receive from

anyone except me. So? How?"

"Well, it's like scrying."

"You mean crystal-gazing?"

"Just about."

"I don't believe it."

"Why not? We come out of a crystal world."

He had to accept that. "How does it work?"

"You don't have to use a crystal ball; anything will serve . . . a pool of ink, water, a mirror, a glass, your fingernail . . . "

"Yes?"

"I used your computer screen and concentrated on it. You have to lose yourself into something."

"And?"

"The screen seemed to turn milky, then black, and even the reflections on it faded."

"And?"

"Then I saw you, in black and white, not moving, like a still photograph."

"Yes?"

"Then color came and you began moving, the way you pace while you're talking and thinking hard. It was like a film slowly starting."

"Did you hear me?"

"Not at first. It was silent. Then I began to hear your voice. And then it wasn't a movie on the screen anymore, it was real. It was like I was standing at the side of the room and you were in the center, and you looked at me, and I went to you and—and you held me and—and I was with you inside the computer."

"How could you be sure it was me? Most people complain that I'm so changeable, adaptable, that there isn't any real bedrock me . . . Even my first wife."

She compressed her lips and looked like a criminal required to convict herself. Then, "You're not going to like this, darling, and I'd rather not tell you, but . . . Well, you're deep and complex and adaptable and moody and—but not all that mysterious to a Titanian. That's why so many of us prefer living on Terra; you're sort of simple arithmetic to us and it makes life so much easier. So I was able to re-create your person and personality . . . "

She was right, he didn't like it at all, but he controlled himself. "So you went in. As what? 'Bits' in the memory banks?"

"We can transform into any living thing, from an amoeba to a brontosaur. There's a living organic switchboard in your tank, a Pons Varolli which is the control station for coordinating your sensations as it receives them. I duplicated it and joined it in parallel."

"Kind of a backup Pons?"

"Just about."

"And you were alive and well in the tank, sustained by the same nutrients that feed it?"

"Yes. A freeloader. I apologize."

"And accessible only to me?"

"Only to you."

"Then how could that damned Manchu Duke of Death have found out where you were holed up?"

"I'm not sure. He's brilliant, a rare Mensa type. and he may have deduced it. Or his devoted exo-computer may have squealed."

"It knew?"

"They all knew. Your tank is in touch with all the other organics within reach."

"How?"

"Crosstalk and sidebands of communication signals and power lines. I learned a lot in your tank."

"And you were safe. Why the hell didn't you let me know?" His anger wasn't as controlled as he imagined. "My God, I nearly went out of my mind worrying about you."

"But I did. I did! Every tank in the network was sending the message."

"What message?"

"That I was safe. Didn't you get it?"

"I got nothing. What'd you send?"

"That I was okay."

"The only okays I got were from the zoo and a bank and a consulate."

"What were they?"

"That your psycat could share half a cage—that the bank could only allow me half the money I wanted—that a half-year visa permit for Triton was okay. Wait a minute. Yes. Also that I could share half a cabin on the jet to Ganymede."

"What did the computers say? Exactly?"

"One-half O.K. The 'half' was the printed number."

"Oh Rogue, Rogue, darling Rogue! Where were your wits?"

"Planning the Triton hit. For your sake."

"Yes, yes, and thank you, my love, thank you. But. Well . . . What's a small cup of coffee? A half cup? Or, what's a half-man-half-god?"

"Why, a demitasse, of cour—" His voice faltered. "And. A. Demi. God . . . ? Oh jeeze! Sweet
jigjeeze! So it was 'Demi O.K.' all along. Demi
from the French for half." he burst out laughing,
all anger gone. "I'm the world's prize ass."

"You had more important things on your mind."

"But I should have—" he sputtered. "I, *Ich, Moi*,
the late, great synergist, to miss an obvious clue
like that! How the mighty have fallen."

"Not in my eyes."

"Oh you! You're queer for me. But why didn't
you use your name in the message, love?"

"And announce it to the world? The code was
specified only for you, FWO, For Winter Only, in
the command sent out to the network."

"Only for me? Then how did the Duke of Death
know you were safe, and a computer could tell me
where?"

"His tank must have overridden the command
and released it to him. Apparently the Manchu's
loving trick is a blabbermouth."

"Trick? Ah-ha! So you know about that sick fag
scam too, eh?"

"Us tanks know everything."

"How'd you know the hassle was cooled and it
was safe to come out? The network again?"

"Nig Englund's zoo tank input all. I must say,
darling, what you did to To-ma Yung was so
fiendish that I'm a little scared of you."

"Not such a simple arithmetic clown after all?"

"Oh, I *did* hurt you!" She reverted to the
original Demi of *Solar Media,* frightened and on
the verge of tears. "I knew it would, but what
could I do? You had to have an answer and I had to

tell the truth. You'd have seen through any lie and been twice as angry. Please, Rogue, try to understand. Please? Rogue? Friends?" She stuck out a hand and began to resemble a trustworthy, loyal, naked girl scout.

He looked at the hand, at her tortured face, suddenly grinned, leaped up and dashed into the workshop. He returned almost immediately and sat down again alongside her. She hadn't changed her pose or expression. She seemed frozen in anguish.

"Since you and the computer fantasized about it so erotically," he said, "we might as well make it real." He slid the pink-gold seal ring onto the third finger of her left hand. "Want me to light a fire, love? I don't know whether there's any champagne in the fridge."

She looked at the ring, squealing, every inch the Virginia debutante. "Oh Rogue! Rogue! Rogue!" She flung herself on him and smothered his mouth with hers.

He accepted his reward with pleasure, then, "R. Ls gtbd. Cmn Stsp." He freed his lips. "Right. Let's go to bed. Come on, Starsprite."

But her muffled adoration had turned to muffled pain and surprise.

"Demi! What is it? What's wrong?"

"Ex-excuse m-me," she faltered, "but I think I'm going to shell a pea."

"What!"

"I think so."

"It's only two months."

"Yes, b-but . . . "

"And you don't show anything up front."

"Yes, b-but it's all new and different. The f-first time ever. I . . . I seem to be b-breaking all the rules of civilized warfare."

"Holy saints preserve us! I'll call Odessa. Don't move. Don't do anything." He raced to the phone, wildly excited. "Another brand-new pattern, by God! Another brand new crisis. Never a dull moment with a Titanian. I wonder what in the world we're going to prod—Hello, Odessa? Rogue Winter here. Help!"

○   ○   ○

Odessa Partridge here. I began this lunatic love story, so I'll wrap it up.

We're holding the Manchu in strict secrecy for several reasons. One of them is that he's burned out, as Nig Englund warned, and we're trying an interesting experiment. You know how patients with failed livers are attached to an *apparat* which restores their blood. We're trying to restore the Manchu's mind the same way, using dolphins.

They're very bright, perhaps more so than most humans, and we link them with the Duke in neural series and run a cerebral charge through them. We're hoping that the dolphin's circuits will open up the Manchu's; he's too brilliant to waste.

Perhaps I'd better explain that for the types who just switch on a lamp and don't ask any questions. I'll use Xmas tree lights as an example. When they're wired in parallel you have a pair of lines coming from the outlet, and each bulb is connected to both these parallel lines, like this:

O   O   O   O

When a string of lights is wired in series they're like a string of beads. A single line passes the current through each bulb in turn and they all light up when the circuit is completed:

——O——O——O——O——

We did this with the dolphins and the Duke; he's the final brain in the series. Of course, if and when he recovers his marbles he may start thinking like a dolphin and take to the sea, and if he turns deadly again the fishing industry may be in for a hard time.

While we're holding the Manchu, the Meta negotiations with Triton promise to turn realistic. Oparo and his Merry Mafia aren't too happy about that, and Jay Yael is struggling to cool it. I had to send Barb back to Ganymede to help. Incidentally, she pulled off a coup; she enlisted Winter's teeny-zapper for Intelligence training. That young demon will make one hell of a *Garda* op.

The Titanian sprite was right; she shattered all the rules. She gave birth to a pair of twin boys without any trouble, just shelled them out like peas. They weighed five pounds each, ten pounds in all, and she never showed it, before, behind, between, above or below. And how could she have produced ten pounds (10) of hybrid in two months (2)? The Solar Medical Association is panting to get at her and them, particularly because the boys are fully developed and don't need incubation.

They're perfectly normal, conventional Terran kids; nothing Titanian about them, we all thought, and their mum and dad are perplexed by that . . . secretly disappointed, I think. They're not fraternal, they're identical twins named Tay and Jay, and they're tagged with anklets so we can tell them apart. However, they're not completely, absolutely, one-hundred-percent identical.

You may recall Cluny Decco's mentioning that she and Damon Krupp had been monitoring the dreams of their experimental baby while it was undergoing the maser generated fetal amplification by syndetic emission of radiation which resulted in Rogue Winter. We did the same with his and Demi's kids as soon as they were born, and discovered that they were isomers, mirror-image twins, which is unusual but by no means unique.

People often wonder what a fetus could possibly dream about. After all, they have no material, no experiences to draw on. The answer is the "cultural unconscious." They're charged with the eons of cultural accumulation which went into the development of modern man, and they think and dream in these powerful evolutionary surges.

Exempli gratia: all of us, at one time or other, have been attacked by a vague fear, an unaccountable terror without any source or object. Psychiatrists try to rationalize this in terms of inhibitions and insecurities, but the truth is this is a blind surge out of our collective deposits, a bequest from Stone Age generations who survived on the fear of the unknown.

On the other hand, birth is a shocking experience for a creature that has been cloistered in a womb, and provides ample material for its bewildered dreams. It did for Demi's twins and this is how we discovered that they were dextro and levo mirror-images. Their confusions were bonded together by "c," the symbol for the speed of light and also, today, the multivalent speed of concept. Their thoughts were sometimes specific, other times inchoate, and curiously rotated to the right and left:

Jay, the dextro

AcA
CAcAC
SHOcK
cONTACT
cACOPHONY
cONFLICT
SHOcK
CAcAC
AcA

Tay, the levo

AcA
CAcAC
KcOHS
TCATNOc
YNOHPOCAc
TCILFNOc
KcOHS
CAcAC
AcA

Philosophers today sometimes suggest that the true reading of $E = Mc^2$ should be, "Evolution is equal to Man multiplied by the speed of concept raised to the second power."

All normal and serene, yes? Except that I dropped in today to keep an eye on the staff, as promised. (Demi's taken Rogue on his first visit to Virginia, to show her conquest off with pride, I'm sure.) Then I had a look at the kids in their bassinets. Damn if Jay, the righty, wasn't clutching at a crib rail with his left hand, and Tay, the lefty, was clutching with his right. I checked their I.D. anklets to make sure. Yep, no doubt of it, they'd reversed their roles. I had to let them know that I knew they were doing a number.

"Hey! Smartass kids, wake up," I said. "This is your powerful godmother grilling you. You may not be able to speak but I'm damn sure you half-pint prodigies can hear and understand. You've transformed and switched, haven't you? Jay's become Tay, and vice versa. Very funny. Very funny."

The tiny Terranian devils rolled over on their backs and gave me such a look of gay mischief that I couldn't help laughing.

Naughty baby deceivers, half Terran, half Titanian, and God only knows which half of which will be up to what! The Sprite and the Synergist have one hell of a brand-new pattern on their hands. So does the Solar.